Night Terrors

Without warning, the shadow ducked and seemed to dissolve into the thick darkness. I watched the closed door, guessing whoever it was would try to escape now that I'd spotted him. But the door didn't open. I heard fumbling sounds from my bedside table.

Quickly I pushed myself up from the bed... I didn't know what I was going to do for sure, but I wasn't going to stay in the room with an intruder. Planning to get out first, then block the doorway while I screamed for help, I dived for the door.

My fingertips barely brushed the cool metal of the doorknob before something heavy and hard crashed down on my head. I can't say that I saw stars like in the cartoons, but there was a brilliant, almost pretty explosion of light before everything went dark.

More heart-stopping Nightmares...

The Dark Visions Trilogy *L. J. Smith*
1. The Strange Power
2. The Possessed
3. The Passion
The Substitute *Robert Hawks*
Room Thirteen *T. S. Rue*
The Teacher *Joseph Locke*
Deadly Stranger *M. C. Sumner*
Vampire Twins *Janice Harrell*
1. Bloodlines
2. Bloodlust
3. Bloodchoice
4. Blood Reunion

NIGHTMARES

NIGHT TERRORS

Nicole Davidson

HarperCollins*Publishers*

First published in the USA in 1994 by Avon Books.
First published in Great Britain 1996
by HarperCollins*Publishers* Ltd.,
77-85 Fulham Palace Road, Hammersmith, London W6 8JB

1 3 5 7 9 8 6 4 2

ISBN 0 00 675225 X

Printed and bound in Great Britain by
Caledonian International Book Manufacturing Ltd, Glasgow

To Ellen Krieger, my wise editor—
for seeing both the best
and the worst in a story . . .
and knowing how to make it come out right,
for loving a good mystery,
for believing in Nicole Davidson—

My deepest thanks,
N.D.

prologue

As always, the nightmare began innocently enough. I was walking down a long, brightly lit corridor crammed with people. The place looked like the inside of a school or a big office building. I had no real sense of who I was . . . or maybe I did know, deep down somewhere. But I knew I wasn't Maggie Johnson, sophomore at Andrew Wilkens High in Winona, Minnesota.

I walked slowly down the hallway, humming to myself, and people turned to smile at me.

"How are you today?" they asked, very friendly and relaxed-sounding, as if they knew me.

"Fine," I said. My voice sounded cheerful, but I had to fake my answering smile because I didn't recognize any of them. They were all strangers.

As I squeezed between people clogging the hall, I felt as if I were searching for something. Maybe I'd lost a hair ribbon, a library book, or my purse. I couldn't remember what it was.

Nevertheless, a tight, pinching feeling of urgency built inside my chest, as though I *had* to find whatever it was I'd misplaced . . . or something terrible would happen to me.

I walked faster, peering down intersecting corridors, but they were empty and dark. The smiling people disappeared, and I was alone.

Now I didn't dare look behind me. I knew, as I always knew from the icy fear that numbed the corners of my soul, what was following me.

1

A second set of footsteps echoed behind mine.

I began to jog down the hall, which became a tunnel that grew darker and darker the farther I went.

Suddenly, a bone-grating scream filled my ears, and I clapped my hands over them, trying to block out the terrible sound. But it was no use. I could hear *her* through my fingers.

"Stop! Come back here!" she screeched furiously.

Although I couldn't make out any more of her wild shouts, I understood that it was me she was after.

I ran as fast as I could, my legs churning, my shoes slipping on the waxed institutional tiles as I rounded a dim corner. At last I couldn't resist any longer; I had to look over my shoulder to see how close she was.

I turned my head and let out a wail of terror. She was only a few feet behind me, almost within an arm's length.

Her eyes were stretched wide and bright with blood lust. Her mouth gaped open in another wail. "I'll kill you! I'll rip you to shreds!" she screamed.

Her hair was wild and electric, standing out all around her head as she tore after me—sort of like the sketch of the monster Medusa after Perseus chopped off her snake-haired head in Edith Hamilton's *Mythology*. Most terrifying of all, something sharp and shiny gleamed in her clenched hand.

If she caught me, my life would be over! I knew that as surely as I knew my own name.

The tunnel grew tighter—pitch black and steamy. My lungs burned so painfully from running, I could hardly breathe. Unable to force my parched tongue and lips to work right, I could only croak out a last futile protest as I raced on.

"Stay away! Please, oh please, leave me alone!"

Just ahead loomed an enormous door. It looked much too big for me to open. But I quickly reached up over my head, grabbed the knob, and pulled with all my strength.

2

It didn't budge at first, and I felt the crazy woman's hot breath on the back of my neck. I sensed that it would be only a matter of seconds before her wicked blade sliced between my ribs, spilling out my life in bloody waves across the floor.

I fiddled frantically with locks, chains, bolts . . . and finally the door swung inward. Bursting into the night, I gasped as the cold air smacked me in the face, hitting me so fiercely it stung with each sharp blast.

At last, my eyes popped open. I stared around me, disoriented and terror stricken, my cheeks hot and puffy, my lungs heaving desperately for air. And I looked up to see my father standing in front of me, his hand raised from having slapped me awake.

"Oh, Daddy!" I cried, throwing myself into his arms. "It happened again. The dream . . . it was awful!"

He gave me a quick, reassuring hug, then pulled away. His face looked haggard and gray beneath the dark shadow of his whiskers. For a second, I wondered how much sleep he ever got, always half-listening during the night for the moment when I'd leap from my bed.

Slowly I realized where we were—in the middle of the front lawn of the brick apartment house where we lived. I leaned back against a rotting maple that almost filled the little patch of dried-up grass between concrete sidewalk and driveway.

"I got out of the house again!" I sobbed.

"I know, but you're all right now. Come inside," he said, looking warily up and down the street, as if afraid the neighbors would see us and think he'd done something wrong.

With so many ugly stories in the news about abused kids, someone who didn't know us might think he'd been beating me when he slapped my face. But if he hadn't done something drastic to wake me up, I might have run into the street or dream-acted something else just as dangerous, and hurt myself really badly. It wouldn't have been the first time.

"I can't go back to sleep," I groaned. Tears streamed down my face, but I was too exhausted to wipe them away.

"We'll turn on the TV. I'll stay up with you and we can watch some dumb old movie." He smiled, but his eyes were red and swollen with fatigue.

"No, Dad," I said. "You need to get some rest. It only comes once in a night. I'll be okay now. Really. I just don't feel like sleeping."

He nodded grimly and followed me into the house, then locked the door after us—the entry lock in the knob, a mammoth brass dead bolt, and two chains, one high and one low. They weren't there to keep out burglars. They were supposed to keep me in.

one

"Hey, Maggie!"

I turned to see Elly Reardon streaking through the language-arts wing toward me. I smiled at her even though the three-hour nap I'd grabbed before getting ready for school hadn't done much to rest me.

"What's up?" I asked.

"I have a massively super, incredible, brilliant idea!" she cried. "Since it's Friday, why don't you stay over at my house tonight? We can pick up a couple of videos, nuke some popcorn, and have a party—just the two of us!"

"I'm moving out of town in a few days. I don't feel like celebrating," I grumbled.

She frowned, her long, permed hair spritzing off at funny angles around her high cheek bones. "It's not like a celebration. More like a good-bye night. We need to do something special together, just you and me."

"I don't feel like it," I snapped.

She got quiet and bit down on her lower lip, blinking at me through teary eyes. "Sometimes you're a rotten friend, Maggie Johnson," she choked out.

Shutting my eyes, I took a deep breath as she dashed off toward the Exit sign. *I can't do this to her*, I thought guiltily. But I'd never, ever told anyone about my dreams. They'd think I was nutsoid! Heck, *I* thought I was cracking up, why shouldn't they?

I clutched my books to my chest and ran after her.

We were outside and halfway across the parking lot to the cinder track that looped the football field before I caught up with her.

"Listen!" I gasped. "I can't stay over. I don't do sleepovers."

Elly glared at me. "You told me you don't like pajama parties. That's cool. Some kids don't like crowds, stupid games, and stuffing their faces with ice-cream sundaes until they puke. But this is just you and me! I thought we were best friends!"

"We are!" To prove it I draped my arm around her shoulders and gave her a squeeze. "Of course we are," I said over the lump in my throat.

"But you're moving to Ohio! I may never see you again!"

My move was probably harder for Elly than it was for me. After all, I'd been moving every year or so for all of my life. We'd been in Winona for almost eighteen months. That was about as long as my dad had ever kept a job.

It always happened suddenly. He'd get a lay-off notice from the factory or warehouse where he was working. He'd scout around, but finally come home one night saying there was nothing else for him nearby. So we'd have to pack up, sometimes that very night because he was so worried about being out of work, and drive on to some other small town where he could find a new job. He had the worst luck with jobs I'd ever heard of.

Although I'd lost tons of friends because of our constant moves, I'd gotten used to people flitting in and out of my life. My mom and dad were the only ones who were always there for me; my grandparents had died before I was born, and there were no aunts, uncles, or cousins. As soon as we settled into a new town, I'd write to my old friends, giving them my address and phone number. But they never wrote back, and almost never called. After a while, I stopped blaming them for breaking their promises.

6

Maybe it was easier that way. I stopped missing them a lot sooner than I would have if they'd written. And I'd learned to make new friends quickly.

"This is different," I assured Elly. "We won't lose each other."

"Because I'll write," she said with rock-hard determination.

I winced at the familiar words. "More than that— because we'll both have our licenses by summer. Every school vacation we can visit whenever we want," I said brightly, beginning to feel a little better. "I won't have to ask my folks to drive me, I can just borrow the car and come!"

"But," she reasoned, "you can't drive all the way from Ohio and back in one day."

My smile wavered.

"You'll have to stay over . . . at least for one night."

I swallowed and looked away from her across the field to the track where the cross-country team was doing laps, where Elly was supposed to be right now.

She reached over and touched my arm. "What's wrong, Maggie?"

I shook my head, the words clogging in my throat as I pulled away. "You'd think I was weird if I told you."

"I could never think anything bad about you."

"No!" I said sharply. "You don't understand! If I tell you, you won't want to be my friend any more."

"That's ridicul—" She broke off at the enraged expression on my face and let out a deep breath. "It's that serious, huh? Well, look at it this way—you have nothing to lose."

"What's that supposed to mean?"

"You're moving hundreds of miles away. We won't get to see each other except a couple of times each year. If I hate your guts because of something major freaky you did . . . well, it's not like we have to face each other every day."

I shifted my feet a couple of times and looked around

nervously. "You're right. But I don't want to talk here."

Maggie glanced at her cross-country coach. Mrs. Cheney was staring daggers at her from across the football field.

"I really, really have to go now," she said. "But I'll drop by your place on my way home, okay?"

"Yeah," I muttered, feeling sick to my stomach. I still didn't want to tell her, but I couldn't let her think I didn't like her anymore just because I was moving.

We took a bag of Oreos and a quart of milk upstairs to my bedroom and sat on the bed. As I munched on the rich, fudgy cookies I watched Elly's eyes wander about my room.

"You've been packing," she commented, a catch in her voice.

"I had to start sometime."

"Looks like you're almost done."

I shrugged. I'd gotten real good at packing. Besides, there never was all that much to take. Mom and Dad didn't have money for expensive clothes or elaborate games and stereo equipment for me. And my mother was a neataholic. Anything we didn't absolutely need got picked up by Goodwill.

"Well," Elly said with a sigh, "I guess you'd better get it over with."

"I guess so," I muttered, lifting the milk carton to my lips for a long, fortifying swig. I let the cold liquid stream down my throat, then thrust the carton at her.

She started to drink.

"I have bad dreams," I blurted out.

Elly choked on the milk and sputtered white bubbles between her lips. "You have dreams?" she laughed. "Everyone dreams."

"Not like me," I said solemnly. "I have nightmares. And not the kind that most kids have, about walking naked into Algebra class, or falling down an endless dark hole like Alice in Wonderland, or having to kiss

8

a whiskery Aunt Kate at Christmas. These are horrible dreams, dreams I can't wake up from."

"You're kidding."

She looked more curious than afraid for my sanity. In a way that was reassuring. But then I thought, Elly's always been a little ditzy; maybe it just hasn't sunk in yet.

I went on. "Sometimes I jump out of bed and run through the house screaming, knocking over lamps, fighting to get out through the front door." I watched her expression for signs of weakening loyalty.

She squinted at me as if trying to understand a hard math problem. "Like sleepwalking, only doing the 40-yard dash?"

In spite of myself, I grinned at her. "You jerk . . . not like a race . . . like if I stop running, I'll *die!* I mean it. I know that if I stop, whatever's chasing me will kill me."

Elly put down the cookies and milk on my night table. "You're serious? You have these weird dreams every night?"

"No. But if I let myself relax and go deeply to sleep, it usually happens."

She frowned in concentration. "I did a science fair project on sleep stages for seventh grade. Deep sleep . . . that's called the REM state."

"What's REM mean?" I figured she didn't mean the rock group.

"It's the brain-wave level where your most vivid dreams occur. REM stands for Rapid Eye Movement. When you reach that stage, your eyes sort of flit around even though your eyelids are closed."

"Well, maybe I'm normal that way, but these aren't ordinary dreams. I told you, I can't escape from them. Sometimes Mom or Dad can't even wake me up, and I get out of the house before they can stop me. Like last night."

"Oh, geez, Maggie—that's creepy!"

I nodded.

9

"Have you ever been to a doctor?"

I was feeling both restless and exhausted now. I couldn't sit still any longer. Pushing up off of my bed, I crossed the room to the brass bookcase I'd had for as long as I could remember. I sat on the floor and started pulling books off of it and shoving them into a box.

"Has a doctor ever examined you?" Elly repeated. "You know, to find out if there's something physically wrong with you."

"Sure . . . doctors at the emergency room of whatever hospital was nearest to us. One time, my dad had to take me to the ER because I'd run into the road and got hit by a car."

Elly let out a soft gasp and came over to sit on the floor beside me. "It's a miracle you're alive," she whispered hoarsely.

Shaking my head, I shrugged. "It wasn't that bad. I only broke my arm. The car was stopping at a light. I think I ran into it, more than it ran into me."

"That doesn't matter!" she cried out, sounding angry. "What if it had been doing sixty?"

"Then I guess I wouldn't be here talking to you."

She huffed at my nonchalance. "What else?" she asked in a tone that said, *Well, we might as well get it all out while we're at it!* "What else happened?"

"I broke through a second-floor bedroom window when I was seven years old. By the time I hit the front lawn, I was awake. But there were cuts from the glass all over my arms and face."

"Wow," she breathed.

Bending toward her, I pulled back my short brown bangs and showed her the faint pink two-inch scar high on my forehead.

"You got that from the glass?"

"Yeah." I dropped my hands and stared down at them. "The doctor in the ER that night asked me what happened, and I told him about the nightmares. Usually I didn't talk about them to anyone. If I got hurt, I just said I was klutzy—I'd fallen down stairs or something. But he was nice and didn't rush me, even though there were other people waiting for him to take care of them."

"So? What did he say about the dreams?"

"He said they were called night terrors—really bad dreams that are hard to shake. But he said I'd probably outgrow them in a couple of years, by the time I reached puberty."

"But you didn't."

A wave of nausea swept through my stomach. "No."

Elly began taking books slowly from the shelf and placing them into the box. "That's why you always look so tired. You don't get any sleep," she commented, as if putting puzzle pieces together in her mind.

"I sleep two or three hours at a time," I explained. "I can usually keep myself from drifting off too deep. I get up and walk around the house, watch TV, drink coffee, then rest an hour or so."

"And I thought you were just naturally a workaholic or something. I thought you were worn out because of being entertainment chairman for Student Council, sophomore class correspondent for the school newspaper, community volunteer coordinator for the HELP Project, and in charge of recycling for the whole school."

I smiled at her. "Well, wouldn't doing all that make *you* tired?"

"Sure. But you do all those things to keep busy, too busy to sleep or think about the nights . . . right?"

"Yeah," I said. "Keeping busy is what I do best. Thinking is a bad scene, almost as bad as sleeping."

My stomach was hurting worse now. A dull fatigue pain settled behind my forehead, and my eyes burned as if acid had splashed in them. But that was normal for me. A three-hour nap wasn't enough to keep anyone going for a whole day.

"Hey, how about a cup of coffee?" I suggested, trying to be cheerful.

"Naw. I *want* to dream tonight."

11

"About Sean?" I teased.

For once she didn't punch me in the arm when I mentioned Sean Stevens's name. "He *is* awfully nice. I think he might ask me to Homecoming."

"I hope he does," I said softly.

I'd miss Homecoming at Andrew Wilkens High this year. Of course, I'd be in a new town with new friends. If I worked fast, maybe I'd go to Homecoming in Dayton. At any rate, I felt better now that we'd finished talking about the terrors and were back to gossiping about normal things.

"Listen," Elly said, leaning forward and speaking softly, "*please* come over Friday night. We'll stay up all night if you want, just watch one video after another, eat popcorn, and talk."

"I don't know," I said with a sigh. "What if I fall asleep?"

"I'll be there to make sure you don't hurt yourself."

"That's . . . that's not the only thing I'm worried about," I stammered, looking her in the eye.

She frowned. "I don't understand."

"What if I *hurt* you?" It was my worst fear, worse than the thought of never waking up and dying at the hands of the mad woman who chased me. I did violent things while I was caught up in a terror. What if I attacked my mother or father, or a friend who was trying to protect me from injuring myself?

"You wouldn't hurt me," Elly said with conviction. "We're the best friends ever. Nothing will come between us. Nothing."

two

We dragged a ton of stuff down the stairs into Elly's basement—enough food to feed the entire Student Council, sleeping bags, pillows, her CD player and collection of discs, and the three videos we'd picked up at Video Mania an hour earlier.

I stood in the middle of the rec room and glanced around. It was already after seven o'clock. But down here, the only way I could tell it was night was by looking at the two small, rectangular panes of glass high up on the paneled walls. No sun shone through; they were a solid black.

Like a lot of houses in Elly's neighborhood, the basement was mostly underground. The only door leading directly outside opened into a cement stairwell that climbed up to a metal storm-cellar door in the backyard.

I watched Elly trudge up the stairs and lock the outside door, then come back down and latch the inside one.

"Satisfied?" she asked.

"Since I'm not familiar with your house, my subconscious might not remember details, like the location of doors," I said hopefully. But there were the other stairs up to the Reardons' kitchen.

Elly followed my gaze. "We can push my mom's sewing cabinet in front of the stair bottom," she suggested. "That way you'd have to climb over it to get to the steps."

13

"It doesn't matter. I'm not going to fall asleep tonight," I assured her.

She sat down and put on her favorite CD—a new one by Grief Relief. Even if I hadn't liked their music, I'd have listened to them because their name was cool. I squatted down beside her, listened, and hummed along with the melody while flipping through the rest of her CDs. She didn't say anything for more than fifteen minutes—which was unusual for her.

"What are you thinking?" I asked at last.

She sighed. "About what you said a while ago . . . about not falling asleep tonight. You know, it might not be a bad idea if you *did* have one of your dreams."

I glared at her. "Yeah, right. Just like it'd be good for me to drink a gallon of turpentine!"

"Really," she insisted, facing me with an excited sparkle in her pretty eyes. "The only way to figure out why you keep having these nightmares is by understanding what they mean."

"Give me a break, Dr. Freud," I muttered, reaching for a handful of potato chips.

"I'm serious. I told you about my science fair project. For my research, I had to read tons of articles about dreams. Most dreams have something to do with our real lives. They show we're anxious about something. But they're in a kind of code."

"I told you, my dreams are nothing like other people's—"

Elly shook her frizzy blonde head stubbornly. "Whether you realize it or not, you're afraid of something, or something is bothering you. It's coming out in your dreams because you can't face it in real life."

"That's ridiculous!" I said, laughing a little too loudly. "I have a great life! Lots of friends, decent grades in school, and my mom and dad are one of the few couples in the world who aren't splitting up . . . there's nothing I can't handle."

"Nothing you *know* of," Elly said, shaking her finger at

14

me. "The key to getting rid of nightmares is remembering your dream and decoding it. Once you figure out what's been eating at you all these years, you can work out your fears and the dreams will go away!"

"Simple as that," I muttered skeptically.

"It might take some time, but I bet we could figure it out together."

I stared at her. "I told you, there's no way I'm going to let myself fall asleep tonight."

Elly shrugged, then quickly jumped up. "Fine. But I'm going to be prepared just in case." She scrounged around in a desk and came away with a pen and note pad. "If you do fall asleep, I'll wake you up after you've been dreaming for a few minutes. I'll be able to tell when you reach REM by the movements under your eyelids. Then you can tell me exactly what happ—"

"No!" I shouted.

"I'll wake you up before it gets bad. Promise! And I won't let you out of the house."

I knew that she was just trying to help, but she didn't understand. Lately, it was taking more and more to wake me from my dreams. The wild woman came closer, and her screams echoed in my ears so loudly I couldn't hear my mother or father shouting for me to wake up. Sometimes even their shakings weren't enough to rouse me. Besides, if my sleeping mind perceived Elly as part of the threat, I might lash out at her.

I reached for the extension phone on the coffee table.

"What are you doing?" Elly asked.

"Calling a couple of friends to come over and help me stay awake."

"I thought you didn't want people to know—"

"I don't, and they won't. You have to swear to me you won't say anything about the night terrors. As far as our friends are concerned, they'll just be here to party with us."

She watched me suspiciously. "Who are you calling? I don't want Diane and Meghan over here. They're boring,

15

and besides, this is supposed to be *our* night."

"I'm not calling them." I smiled at the look of horror that spread across her face as she watched me punch in the numbers.

"You're not!" she cried, diving for the phone. "You wouldn't, Maggie!"

I jumped to my feet and danced away from her with the receiver in my hand. "Hey, Sean!" I cried into the mouthpiece. "Doing anything special tonight?"

It was two in the morning when I heard something I'd never heard at my house.

"Hey, you girls had better get some sleep!" Mr. Reardon shouted down the stairs to the basement. "Boys, head on home now."

"Yes, sir," Sean said, leaping three feet away from Elly at the sound of her father's booming voice.

They'd been snuggling on the couch for the past four hours, gazing into each other's eyes and kissing more than watching the movies. I laughed at Sean as he stared up toward the kitchen; every ounce of blood had drained from his face.

"I don't think he's coming down," I said.

Paul Hunter pushed up off the floor where he'd been sitting beside me. "I guess we should leave anyway."

Paul had come along with Sean to even up the boy-girl ratio. For a senior, he was pretty nice. We'd talked about school a lot, but didn't even hold hands during the romantic scenes of the movies. He wasn't my type, whatever that was. Paul was easygoing, got B's and C's in school, liked everyone, and everyone liked him because there was nothing to dislike about Paul. He just wasn't terribly exciting.

"Thanks for inviting us over," Sean murmured dreamily to Elly.

"Thanks for coming," she whispered between their tenth and eleventh good-bye kisses.

"Hey guys, remember me?" I said, tapping Elly on the

shoulder. "I was the one who made the phone call."

"I don't think they're tuned in to your wavelength," Paul suggested when neither of them responded.

"Guess not," I agreed, turning my back on them to say polite, good-night things to Paul. "I hope you weren't too bored. The movies were pretty cool at least."

"I had a great time," he insisted.

"It was sort of hard to tell," I said. "You don't laugh at the funny parts or say much of anything while the movie's on."

He shrugged. "I guess I'm just thinking too hard about what's happening."

Elly and Sean were at last winding up their passionate farewells.

"I'll call you tomorrow," Sean said.

"You mean, today?" Elly giggled.

"Oh yeah, guess it is tomorrow already." He started for the back door, then turned around again to give her one final kiss.

"Good grief," I groaned.

Paul grinned, rolling his eyes as if to say he found the whole thing pretty funny, too. I tried to imagine myself kissing Paul and couldn't.

At last the boys disappeared up the cement stairs. I could hear their voices fading away across the dark backyard. Elly locked up again.

I looked at the clock: 2:20. "So, what do we do now?" I asked. "Watch the rest of the movie?"

Elly sighed happily and collapsed on the couch. She closed her eyes and hugged herself, no doubt imagining Sean's arms still around her.

"Elizabeth Ann Reardon, are you in there?" I shouted in her ear.

She focused on my face unwillingly. "What's your problem?"

"You promised to help me stay awake, remember?"

"I'm sorry." She sat up straight on the couch, trying to appear alert, but her eyelids looked heavy. I began to

17

think I shouldn't have let her talk me into this.

"Maybe I should go home now," I said softly.

"No!" She jumped up. "I'll make us some strong, black coffee. You decide what you want to do next. Maybe we could play Monopoly or cards."

I watched her scramble over the furniture we'd scooted over to block the foot of the stairs and up to the kitchen. A moment later I heard water running and the clink of a teakettle against the stove burner.

I took a deep breath and stretched, then pushed a chair beneath one of the casement windows. Standing on top of the seat, I could just reach the latch to open it. The small glass pane swung up a few inches on the hinge and let in a blast of chilly spring air.

I jogged around the basement, lifting my knees high, drawing gobs of cold oxygen into my lungs. *Good*, I thought, *I'm waking up*.

If I could just make it until six o'clock, I'd talk Elly into walking over to the Pancake House for breakfast and more coffee. After a big stack of pancakes, I'd go home and take a nap in my own bed. A few hours of light dozing would keep me going. I knew a million ways to fight sleep—the deep, dangerous sleep that stalked me.

I'd once tried getting a solid eight hours during daylight, on the theory that night terrors would only visit me during the night. But I'd lapsed into the repeating nightmare then, too. So I knew that simply reversing my sleeping and waking hours wouldn't work.

Elly came down the stairs carrying a red plastic tray with two mugs of coffee and a plate heaped with sugar cookies. I took the coffee but left the cookies for her. Cookies are loaded with carbohydrates, which work like natural sedatives.

"Thanks," I said, sipping from the steaming mug. "This is good. You make better coffee than I do."

She smiled wearily. "My mom buys this gourmet hazelnut blend for company. I snitched some. She won't mind since this is a special occasion."

18

"I think we should watch TV," I said.

"More TV?" she moaned.

"I didn't think you'd mind. You never even looked at the screen during the second movie."

Elly blushed and sipped quickly at her coffee. "I did too."

"Not much," I said, grinning at her. "Did Sean ask you to Homecoming?"

"Not yet. But he's going to . . . I can tell."

I nodded, happy for her.

"I guess TV is okay," she agreed at last, stuffing a few pillows behind her on the couch. "I'm too tired to concentrate on a game."

"You promised," I reminded her.

"I *won't* fall asleep!" she groaned.

I flicked through channels with the remote control. There were a lot of B movies, nothing good. A local, late-night talk show was on. The host and I had become buddies after all the nights we'd spent together. He never landed really good guests, because of the broadcast hour and his irritating habit of slamming everyone. But he kept talking about whatever struck his fancy, and that usually kept me awake.

"How about the *Darrel Burnside Show?*" I asked.

"Anything," Elly agreed with a limp wave of her hand.

I grabbed a book I'd brought along, just in case. At home, I often kept one beside me to pick up at commercials, just to stop my mind from wandering.

Darrel was talking about the dangers of too much sugar in a person's diet. He claimed it lowered your IQ.

"This guy's a real dork," Elly commented over a yawn.

"Yeah, but he's so dorky he's funny," I said. "You should hear him when he gets going on one of his pet peeves, like frozen orange juice."

"I'll bet he's a real scream," Elly commented wryly.

I sat Indian-style on the rec room floor, chuckling every time Darrel said something too dumb to believe.

For a while Elly laughed along, but she sounded like someone who misses the punch line and fakes getting the joke.

After a while, she stopped making any sounds at all.

"Hey, that one was pretty funny!" I said.

No answer.

I turned around to find Elly stretched out on the couch, hugging a pillow, her eyes closed.

"Some help you are," I complained loudly. "Elly, wake up!"

She didn't move.

I reached over and gently shook her shoulder.

"S-S-S-Sean," she murmured blissfully.

"Great. Just great," I muttered.

I suppose if I'd shaken her hard enough she'd have woken up, but I didn't have the heart to interrupt her dream.

I turned up Darrel a little louder and opened my book, bracing my back against the front of the couch for support. Bram Stoker's *Dracula* had always kept me awake in a pinch.

I must have read for a half hour before the rain started. It made a soft, caressing sound against the vinyl siding on the house. Darrel went off the air, replaced by a station call sign. I didn't bother to search out another channel. I'd gotten to the part in the book where Miss Lucy is fading fast, and I was totally into the story.

Some time later, I was sure that I was still reading—at least the familiar words still rumbled through my head— but I felt as if the book was floating in slow motion down into my lap. I had no sense of whether my eyes were open or closed. I no longer knew if I was sitting up or lying down.

A soft dizziness folded around me, as if Dracula's blood-sucking had also stolen my strength to fight morphia. *Sweet morphia,* I thought giddily, *that's what they'd call sleep in a book like this. . . .*

I have to stay awake. I have to stay awake! I told

20

myself, even as my body began to feel as though it were levitating inches above the floor.

Call Elly! a voice inside of me warned.

One good scream would wake her. She'd clobber me until I was completely awake. But I couldn't muster even a little bit of strength to cry out for help.

It was as if one part of me dreaded the nightmare, while another yearned for it . . . like when you drive past a bad automobile accident, and you have to look, because there's this dark side of you hoping for a gory show even while you're saying out loud, "God, I hope no one was hurt."

I wanted to see *her* again, even though I knew she meant to destroy me.

Then I was transported directly to the dark corridor. I searched the length, up and down. Tonight there were no friendly people, no people at all. Maybe I was thinking about our moving away from Winona, secretly worried about being alone even though I never seemed to have trouble scouting up new friends. I found I was able to analyze at least this much of the dream, just as Elly had suggested.

As I moved through the dark, empty corridors, I reached out to touch the walls. They felt like some kind of nonscratch paneling you'd find in an office building. I sniffed the air, and I could smell food cooking— hamburgers maybe, and the sweet, spicy scent of oregano and tomatoes, like in spaghetti sauce. Was I near a restaurant? Then there were other, sharper smells that made me think of the formaldehyde and chemicals in biology lab.

At last the corridor narrowed into the tunnel, and I heard *her* steps coming up behind me. I started running, taking long strides until the tunnel unexpectedly came to an end. Pounding on the wall, I frantically searched with my fingers for an opening between the panels.

The woman's burning breath seared the back of my neck.

"No!" I screamed. "No, no, please leave me alone!"

21

I turned to fight her off, but her face loomed inches from mine, pressing forward. Between us, a knife suddenly appeared, gleaming blindingly.

I tried to shove the woman away, but she kept coming at me, screaming wild things I couldn't understand, brandishing her blade.

Then something cold and wet hit me in the face, and for a second I had a vision of an immense tidal wave crushing down on me.

"Help! Help!" I sputtered, sure I was drowning.

Hands grasped me, hauling me out of the water, brushing away the frigid droplets. . . .

I opened my eyes.

Elly stood in front of me, in the middle of her rec room, an empty glass in one hand, her face distorted with fear.

"I'm okay," I said shakily. "Thanks. I'm okay now." But I couldn't stop trembling.

three

I looked around, gulping down air, my heart racing in my chest. Sweat trickled down inside my blouse, and I clamped a hand over my heart to quiet it and trap the clammy moisture.

"The good news is, I'm still in your basement," I gasped.

"How can you joke at a time like this?" Elly demanded, her face ashen, her eyes bright with fear.

"What else can I do?" I asked. I collapsed on the nearest chair. The muscles in my legs were knotted as if I'd run a very long distance.

"There *must* be a reason for your dreams," she said, sounding like a scientist again. "*Everything* has a reason."

"I don't know . . . ," I murmured. At last my heartbeats were beginning to slow down to a more normal rate. I could breathe without my chest aching. "How long did it last?"

"Probably only five minutes, but it seemed like forever," she admitted grimly. "When I woke up, you were climbing on a chair, trying to reach the window. I tried to talk to you, but it was as if you didn't even know I was there."

I nodded. "Mom used to get spooked because she said my eyes were wide open and I was looking at her, but I didn't recognize her."

"No," Elly said thoughtfully, reaching out for her notepad. "No, it was more like you were looking *through* me . . . into some other world."

I shivered. One of the most terrifying things about the terrors was that I had no memory of seeing anything in the room, including Elly. I'd been lost in another reality. Someday I really might not be able to come back from it!

I dropped my head into my hands. "I must be going crazy."

"Don't say that!" Elly snapped. It was more of an order than something a person said to comfort. "We're going to figure out what's making this happen to you."

"When I was ten years old, the ER doctor said I should have psychiatric counseling. But my parents don't believe in psychiatrists, and treatment like that sometimes takes years. How can we expect to get anywhere in a few days?"

Elly chewed the eraser end of her pencil. "We can at least start. After you're in Ohio, you can call me on the phone, and we can keep talking about your dreams and stuff that might be bothering you."

"Like what?" I demanded.

"I don't know—" She waved me off. "That's not important now. Before you forget, tell me everything you can remember from the nightmare."

I shook my head, stood up, and started pacing the checkerboard tiles of her basement. "It was the same as always, just a few more details get added in each time."

"Like what?"

I squeezed my eyes shut and concentrated. Already the images were drifting away, leaving me feeling calm but exhausted. I knew that now I could safely sleep for a couple of hours without the dream coming back.

"The crazy woman was there, and she was going to stab me with her knife. But before she showed up, I was wandering through the usual long hallways, sort

24

of expecting her . . . or waiting for her." I hesitated. "It was almost as if I *wanted* her to come."

Elly scowled as she wrote on the pad. "Why do you think you wanted her to come?"

"I don't know. . . . I just felt anxious, like when you're waiting for the mail carrier because you're expecting an important letter. I knew she'd come." Another surprising thought struck me. "I needed to see her."

"Why?" Elly asked softly, not looking up from the pad as she scribbled madly. "Why did you need to see her?"

"I don't know." I threw up my hands in frustration and flopped on the couch. "I suppose I've been having the dream so long, I've started expecting her to come. Maybe I figure once she shows, I'll wake up and it'll be over."

Elly shook her head. "That doesn't make sense. Why would you scream and run away if you realized it was just a dream and you'd wake up?"

"You're right." Feeling frustrated, I picked up a potato chip from one of the bowls on the coffee table. The salt tasted wonderful. I ate four more. "I'm always convinced the terror is real. I'm terrified that she's going to kill me."

"What else happens?" Elly asked.

I thought hard. "I can't remember. The more time passes, the less I remember. It's just this vague sense of searching for something. I've lost something, and I can't find it. I don't even know what it is. Then she comes, and I have to run even though sometimes I don't want to. It's as if some force is pulling me on, trying to save me from her."

"Does she ever catch you?"

I thought for a long moment. "Not exactly. It's pretty foggy now, but I can picture her coming up so close I can feel her breath. When I turn around at the very end, her mouth is inches away from me, screaming at me although I can't understand most of the words."

"Does she ever stab you with the knife?"

"I . . . I don't know," I said weakly, shaking my head. "I have a feeling what it will be like if she does. I can almost hear the steel blade grating against my bones and see it cutting into my flesh and spilling out my blood. But I don't know if she ever does it or if I'm just imagining what it might be like."

Elly sighed and laid aside the pad. "You should start writing down everything you can remember as soon as you wake up. Keep a list, and we can talk about it. Sooner or later we'll hit on the reason for your nightmares."

"Night terrors," I corrected her. Somehow, calling them what they were was important to me. A nightmare sounded like something a little kid had. A two-year-old would stagger into her parents' bedroom, wanting to crawl in with them because ugly monsters hid under her bed or lurked in her closet. But I wasn't a little kid any more. I was fifteen years old!

"Tell me what I did," I asked.

"Huh?"

"Tell me everything I did while I was in the terror. My mom and dad won't talk about it. I just wake up and find myself on the front lawn or in a closet. All they say was it was a bad dream."

"Well, I heard you scream—really blood-curdling shrieks," Elly said. She bit her bottom lip and studied me. "That's what woke me up. Then you yelled, 'Get away! Get away from me!' " She hesitated, and I wondered if she was censoring some parts to spare my feelings. "Just before I dumped the water on you, you shouted something like, 'Don't let her get me!' "

Now that she said them, I could almost hear the words coming out of my mouth. "Did it sound like I was calling to you for help?"

"No. More like you were shouting out to anyone who might be around. I grabbed you and tried to shake you awake, but you didn't recognize me. You screamed louder and fought me."

26

"Fought you?" I repeated weakly.

"You, um—" She shrugged, looking away from me.

Then I saw it—the thin streak of blood along one side of her face. I stood up, crossed the room quickly, and bent over to touch the feverish pink welt on her cheek.

"I did that to you?"

Elly pushed my hand away. "You didn't know what you were doing. You were lashing out with your hands, and your fingernail caught me."

"Oh geez, I'm so sorry," I moaned.

"Don't be a dweeb, you didn't know." She studied her hands for a minute. "Can you rest without having another terror?"

"Yeah. But I'll wake myself up in two hours so I won't go under too deep. The dream doesn't usually come back a second time in one night, but I can't be totally sure."

"Don't worry," Elly said, gently touching my shoulder. "We'll find out what's going on with you."

Somewhere deep inside of me, a disturbing doubt slithered in like a beady-eyed snake. What if the truth was worse than the terror? What if I regretted learning the reason for the horrible dreams?

No, I thought. *The truth, no matter how awful it might be, couldn't be that bad.* Could it?

I walked home from Elly's house at nine that morning, after a huge breakfast of pancakes, sausage, applesauce, and milk. Mrs. Reardon made her own applesauce, slicing up apples and sprinkling them with sugar and cinnamon as they simmered soft and fragrant in a pot on the stove. Instead of using syrup, I'd heaped the warm fruit on top of a mountain of fluffy pancakes. I was going to miss her applesauce almost as much as I was going to miss Elly.

And now we had a special bond, one I'd never shared with any other friend. She knew my secret. Even better, she didn't think I was crazy. Somehow that made me feel stronger.

"Maybe she's right," I murmured to myself as I used my key to get into the apartment. "Maybe we can figure out what's giving me the terrors."

Then they'd go away. That would be the best gift in the whole world—eight straight hours of totally dreamless sleep every night.

I walked into the kitchen and caught the trailing end of a conversation between my parents: " . . . don't have any choice. We can't wait," my mother said.

I stared at her, worried by her insistent tone.

She'd always been nervous and pale, sort of hefty, too. Not actually fat, just twenty or thirty pounds bigger than she should have been, even though she tried to diet. She was almost five-foot-eight and big-boned, unlike me. I had stopped growing at five-foot-three and bought my clothes from the petite department. Regular jeans were always too long in the crotch, and skirts that were supposed to end midcalf hung around my ankles. I couldn't put on an extra pound if I killed ten milkshakes a day.

Mom had always said that I resembled my dad's side of the family more than hers. He was short for a man, just her height, and very slim. We had similar, ordinary brown hair, but my eyes were closer to green and his had more gray.

They both turned and stared at me as I stood in the doorway. My mother glanced nervously at him, then turned back to me with a plastic smile on her face. "Hello, sweetie!"

Dad picked up his coffee mug and took a sip while observing me with a dim smile.

"Hi," I said.

Sometimes I wondered if their lives might have been happier if they'd never had me. I knew my wakeful nights tired them out. I suspected that at least a few of the jobs my dad lost had been due to his falling asleep at work, because he'd stayed up all night with me. Maybe, as I got older and stronger, my parents had even gotten

28

a little scared of what I might do to one of them if I went out of control.

"Did you and Elly have fun last night?" my mother asked cheerily. Too cheerily.

I wanted to tell her how awful it had been, but she had enough to worry about these days, what with the move and all. "It was okay," I said. "Is something wrong?"

She shook her head quickly. Her Miss Clairol auburn curls tumbled into her eyes, obscuring them. "No, just the usual." She turned to Dad, as if asking him to explain.

"Our plans have changed a little," he said stiffly. "We've got to leave no later than Tuesday, kiddo. Monday would be even better."

My heart slammed into the wall of my chest. "No!" I cried. "I thought I had a few more days to say good-bye to my friends!"

"I know, sweetie," my mother crooned, rushing to my side. "You'll just have to say good-bye over the weekend. Or maybe you can send your classmates a really nice farewell card."

"Why?" I demanded. "Why do we have to leave so soon?"

"My job," Dad muttered, gazing into his coffee.

"You don't have one," I reminded him bitterly, feeling nasty for rubbing it in but needing to do it anyway.

"I mean," he said slowly, "there's a good chance of my getting one if we reach Dayton by Tuesday. They're interviewing at a tool and die plant." He passed me a weak smile. "You girls have done great with the packing. There really isn't much more to do, no reason to wait. I'll get the U-Haul Sunday night. We can shove off bright and early Monday morning."

I crossed my arms over my chest and glared at him. A possibility leapt into my mind that was almost unthinkable, yet tempting all the same. "What if I didn't go with you?" I asked.

For a long moment no one breathed in the room. A look of anguish flashed across my mom's face, and my dad's hand shook as he lowered his cup to the counter. I felt instantly guilty.

"You *have* to come with us . . . we're your parents," he stated.

"You aren't old enough to be on your own," my mother added quickly.

But I could see what they weren't saying was, *You need us, Maggie. What if the night terrors come and there's no one to stop you from jumping out a fourth-floor window or running in front of a ten-ton truck doing seventy?*

I looked into my mother's eyes, and I could read her fear as clearly as if her face were a neon sign. My father was busy trying not to show any emotion. He turned away from me and looked out the window.

They are terrified for me . . . and maybe even *of me,* I thought again, remembering the bloody scratch I'd left on Elly's cheek.

"I was just kidding," I whispered hoarsely. "I'd never run away or anything like that."

My mother wet her lips with the tip of her tongue. "I'm sorry we have to keep moving like this, sweetie. I wish things had turned out different." Again she cast an apologetic look at Dad, which didn't make much sense because it was his inability to keep a job that kept us on the move. "Someday, maybe," she continued, "it won't be like this. Maybe we'll have a real home where we can put down roots and get to know the neighbors and . . ." She broke into tears.

I walked over and put my arms around her, which wasn't easy, my being so much smaller than she. "It's all right. Come on, Mom. I'll bet we can finish up the packing today."

She sniffled. "You're a good girl, Maggie. You're *my* good girl." She stroked the back of my head.

After a minute, I stepped back from her. "I want to give Elly my new address and phone number, so she can reach me as soon as we're there."

She opened her mouth, then closed it again.

"That's not possible," my father said abruptly. "Getting a phone installed will take at least a week."

"Oh," I said, disappointed. "Then the address?"

"We don't have one yet," my mother said in a low voice.

"You don't even know where we're going to live?" I turned to my father. "I thought you drove to Dayton to check out apartments."

"I did. You saw all the ads I brought back. I've narrowed our choices down to three complexes. They all have openings. I want your mother to choose after she sees them. We can stay in a motel for a night or two."

"But that's expensive," I reminded him.

"So . . . we'll camp out," he said lightly, as if trying to sound like it was all a game. "The weather's getting pretty mild. Doesn't matter, it will only be for a couple of days."

"Once we find a place, you can write to Elly and tell her the address," my mother assured me.

I stared down at my hands, thinking about all the other times I'd written old friends, telling them my new address. Only once had I gotten a letter back. After I wrote back, I received no answer.

Please be different, Elly! my heart cried out. *I need you!*

four

On Monday morning I walked Elly to the bus stop and hugged her good-bye while the driver and other kids looked on. Freddie Merckel, who never kept his mouth shut, stuck his head out the window and shouted something embarrassing about alternative life-styles. Two of the other boys dragged him back inside and punched him in the gut, while the driver looked the other way.

While Elly and I cried on each other's shoulders, everyone else on the bus sat waiting quietly. Finally, she climbed the steps, tears still clinging to her eyelashes. Two of the girls from my recycling committee waved sadly, and Audrey Lyle pushed a little box, tied with a pink ribbon, through the window.

"We were going to give it to you tomorrow at Student Council meeting," she said.

I nodded, unable to speak.

The bus ground its gears, then rattled away. Unwilling to watch it go, I turned away. I didn't want to remember my friends fading into the distance in a cloud of exhaust fumes on a yellow bus.

I stared at Audrey's package.

At last, I started moving back down the sidewalk toward home, untying the ribbon as I walked. Inside was a little gift card signed by everyone on S.C. THANKS FOR YOUR GREAT LEADERSHIP AND MOUNTAINS OF SMILES, it read. GOOD LUCK IN YOUR NEW SCHOOL! With it was a tiny crystal unicorn with a graceful gold horn sprouting from its forehead.

My throat closed up so tightly I couldn't swallow. I blinked back another wave of tears. "Oh fudge," I mumbled. "Why do we have to leave again?"

The worst part was, I had all of my junior and senior years ahead of me. I was afraid I wouldn't even finish high school in the next school. I might be good at adjusting to moves, but it wasn't easy. And I'd have really liked to graduate from Wilkens.

When I got back to the apartment, the U-Haul was out front and Dad was already shoving stuff inside. It was pretty big—not the truck kind, but a long trailer we'd drag behind the car.

"Are you sure the station wagon will be strong enough to pull this thing?" I asked.

"It'll have to be," he said solemnly. "Go help your mother. She's moving everything close to the door so I can load faster."

I sighed and went inside.

By noon we were on the road, but Dad wasn't happy. "We're behind schedule," he fumed, pounding the steering wheel with the heel of his hand. "I knew I should have picked up the U-Haul last night like I'd planned."

"Then it would have been parked out front all night. That's asking for trouble," my mother said.

"What trouble?" I asked.

She hesitated. "The neighbors. They complain about things like that, people with vans or trucks who park them in front of the building. It's an eyesore."

"You worry too much," my father said.

They found something else to argue about before long. Dad was obsessed with making time, and Mom kept saying, "Safe is better than sorry."

"If you're so worried about time, cut straight through Chicago," I suggested, leaning over the front seat to show them on the map. "The route you drew with the red line takes us out of our way."

"That's a good idea," my father said. "We can stay on Interstate 90, right through the city, and save a good hour."

"No!" my mother screeched, clutching his right arm. "Are you crazy?"

I stared at her. "What's wrong with cutting through Chicago?"

"The . . . the crime," she stammered, still staring at Dad. "Carl, it's dangerous. You *know* it's dangerous! Take the long way around."

"It's dangerous *everywhere*," my father said in a low voice.

"Not like in Chicago." She turned to me, maybe hoping I'd talk some sense into him. "There are gangs there, just waiting to pounce on out-of-towners like us. You read about them in the paper. A person's just not safe in a big city any more!"

"You're overreacting again," my father ground out. "Shut up and let me do the driving."

But she didn't shut up. She kept nagging him, trying to get him to take another route, even though he told her he was exhausted and needed to take the shorter route if we were to reach Dayton on schedule.

I got sick of listening to them, rolled up my jacket, and shoved it under my head and against the right rear door. I shut my eyes, wishing I had lids over my ears too, so I could close out their bickering.

The car rumbled soothingly beneath me. The trailer hitch squeaked with each bump in the highway. As we kept exactly to fifty-five miles an hour, staying in the far right lane, everyone else on I-90 swished past us. Dad hated the idea of being stopped by a cop. Even when he was in a hurry, he never went above the speed limit.

I had gotten my usual three hours' sleep plus a nap, but I felt totally wiped out. Elly would say it was emotional strain. She liked to blame everything on the subconscious—from bombing a science quiz to bursting into tears like she had the day when I refused to stay overnight at her house.

The highway sounds were comforting after my tearful goodbyes. I felt myself sinking into a pleasant trance. *Not sleep*, I told myself. *This isn't sleep*. It was daytime, and I wasn't even in bed. It was okay to relax, to just shut my eyes and drift . . .

I was suddenly in *the tunnel*.

Somehow I had skipped the first part of my dream, and I was halfway down the empty, dark tunnel of my terrors.

I was looking for something. I still didn't know what it was.

Then the footsteps started up behind me and quickly grew to a thunderous roar in my ears. Unable to ignore them, I turned. *She* was there . . . chasing after me with her wild hair and gaping mouth. Her eyes were enormous and bright with fury.

"Stop!" she screamed, reaching out toward me. "Come back here! Come back!"

"No! Let me go!" I wailed. I was overwhelmed by a sense of being trapped. Suddenly I found I couldn't run, couldn't escape from the corner I'd been boxed into.

I frantically searched for a handle, a knob, a latch that would release part of the solid wall and let me through to the other side, to safety. I couldn't see her knife, but I knew she must have hidden it somewhere on her, to use as soon as she'd overpowered me. I could feel her hands on me, clutching my clothing, pulling me back.

At last I found a lever, pulled on it, and released a door. I threw myself through the opening.

A fraction of a second before I hit the ground, my eyes flew open and I realized with horror what I'd done.

Black pavement, sliced by a line of yellow paint, rocketed up toward me. Instinctively, I tucked one shoulder to cushion the impact, but I hit the highway hard and streaks of pain shot through me. Car horns blared and brakes squealed. I felt as if every bone in my body had been shattered.

Then there was blessed darkness—no pain, no night terror, nothing . . .

"Call her parents in. She's coming around," a distant voice said.

I kept my eyes shut, wanting to figure out if I was dreaming again before I tried to look. I wondered if dead people dreamed.

Fingers firmly probed my right wrist, my left arm, my ribs. I flinched and whimpered at a sudden, sharp pain through my chest.

"Maggie, are you with us yet?" a friendly male voice asked.

I didn't answer. It might be a trick. Maybe I'd open my eyes and it would be *her*, disguised in men's clothing, talking in a husky voice. Then I remembered the car, and falling asleep, and the highway shooting up to smack me to smithereens.

I opened my eyes to see a man with a narrow face and young, smiling eyes.

"I'm here," I said. "Am I, you know, all in one piece?"

"More or less," he said softly. "You took quite a tumble."

"My mom and dad?"

"They're on their way up from the coffee shop. You were out for quite a while. I sent them down while we worked on you."

"Worked on me?"

He chuckled, snapping off rubber gloves and chucking them into a waste container. A nurse was bustling around, cleaning up bloody tissues and bandage wrappers. She glanced at me once, curiously, then left. I seemed to be in an examination room of some kind, more private than the usual emergency rooms where I'd ended up before.

"You broke your collarbone when you fell out of the car. And you have a couple of cracked ribs. They're going to give you some discomfort for a while. How about I tape them up for you?"

"Thanks," I murmured, still trying to figure out how I'd fallen asleep so fast in the car.

However it had happened, I must have opened the door from the rear seat. Probably the hands I'd felt restraining me were my mom's.

I hated the thought of what I'd put her through. And now Dad had probably missed out on his job.

Looking around, I noticed that someone had put me in a hospital johnny, the paper kind with strings in the back. I still had on my underpants, but nothing else. I sat very still while the doctor started wrapping tape around my ribs, just below my breasts. He stood close enough for me to read his name tag: PETER WINSCHEL, M.D.

"Care to tell me why you bailed out?" he asked in the casual way doctors ask important questions.

I sighed. "Same old thing."

"A fight with your parents maybe?"

"No!" I said quickly.

I didn't want to talk about it, but I sensed that if I didn't, he might get the wrong idea.

"I must have fallen asleep in the backseat. Sometimes I have weird dreams. I think they're real and I . . . I do things."

He stopped wrapping and studied my face. "You sleep-walk?"

I laughed. "More like sleep run, jump, hurdle . . . An ER doctor once told my dad I'd outgrow it. He called the dreams night terrors."

"Really," he said thoughtfully. "So you think you fell asleep, then dreamed something frightening enough to make you open the door and jump out of a moving vehicle?"

"Yeah, weird, huh?" I laughed uneasily, trying to sound amused by the whole thing.

37

"Weird indeed." He frowned at me, not like he was angry, more like he was intrigued with me. "Here at North Central Chicago Hospital," he said slowly, "we have a sleep disorder clinic. I know a young doctor who's done some interesting research on night terrors."

"Well, when she writes her book I want to read it," I said.

"I don't think she'll be publishing anytime soon." He smiled. "But I'm sure she'd like to talk with you."

I squinted at him. "I'm no guinea pig."

"I didn't say you were," he assured me. "I just think she might be able to help you. In return, you may have information she'd find valuable in her studies."

"I . . . I don't know," I said cautiously. "We're just passing through town and—"

Just then Mom burst through the door, followed by Dad. They rushed toward the examination table.

"Are you all right, Maggie?" Without taking a breath or letting me answer, she raced on. "Doctor, is she okay?"

"She appears to be," he said carefully. "Her collarbone is broken. We've set it. The X-rays show cracked ribs and, since they're a little tender for her, I'm taping them up."

"That's all? We can go now?" my mother asked, relief in her voice.

Dr. Winschel looked at me and smiled encouragingly. "I don't think that would be a good idea." He turned back to my parents. "Maggie had a real close call. If she'd fallen out of the left side of the car, she'd almost certainly have been struck and killed by passing automobiles. As it is, she must have landed just right to avoid fracturing her skull. How fast were you traveling?" he asked my father.

"Fifty five, before she—" he hesitated "—before she started pulling at the door handle."

"So you saw that there was a possibility she might fall out, and you slowed down?"

"Right," Dad said. "I must have been going closer to thirty-five when she fell."

The doctor nodded. "That makes sense. Because of the lower speed, she didn't hit with as much force."

"So why can't we leave?" my mother asked, wringing her hands.

"I think it would be better if Maggie spent a night or two here with us," Winschel said firmly.

"That's impossible," my father told him. "I have to be in Dayton today. I was supposed to be there hours ago. My job won't wait."

"Then perhaps you should go on ahead and take care of your personal business while Maggie takes it easy for a while," Winschel suggested. "There's a possibility that she's suffered internal injuries. Internal bleeding can take some time to show up. But if it's there, we'll need to operate immediately."

Mom stared at him, then at me. At last she turned to Dad, fear etched in her features. "She *can't* stay here, Carl."

"I know . . . I know," he muttered. "Look," he said to the doctor, "we don't have any money to pay for a hospital stay. I'm between jobs, and I don't have any insurance. I don't even know how we'll pay the bill for her emergency treatment."

"I see," Winschel said. "Well, it's up to you, of course, but . . ." His eyes shifted slightly, as if he'd thought of something.

"What is it?" I asked.

"I might have a solution." He turned to my father. "I'd like one more physician to look at Maggie. If she says what I think she might, we may have a way to handle the hospital bill for you."

"Really?" My father's face lost a few of its wrinkles. "That would be great, doc!"

I sat in the reception area, trying to hold myself up straight in the chair and take shallow breaths. When I

39

sagged or drew in too much air, pain shot through my ribs like hot lightning.

"Maggie Johnson?" the receptionist called out.

My mother and father stood up beside me. One of them still went with me whenever I had to see a doctor, even though I was fifteen.

This time all three of us walked into an office. There was no examination table, just a big wooden desk with one leather chair behind it and three visitors' chairs in front of it, surrounded by three walls of books. A wide window overlooked a busy Chicago street.

Too restless to sit down again, I stood and stared out the window. Directly below there were buildings that looked like a courthouse and city offices. To their right was a huge store with glistening display windows and a sign. Marshall Field. It appeared that the store filled a whole city block. I must have seen ads for it somewhere. The name made me think of Christmas and pyramids of stuffed animals and elaborate electric train displays.

The door clicked open, and I turned around. A pretty young woman with eager green eyes and pale golden hair knotted on top of her head came in. She smiled at me and nodded politely to my mother and father.

"I'm Dr. Clarice Berman," she said. "I understand Maggie has some interesting nighttime adventures to tell me about."

My mother looked puzzled. "We're not here to talk about bad dreams. That other doctor said my daughter might have internal injuries, and he needed another opinion so she could stay for free."

"I'm afraid you're a little confused," Dr. Berman said calmly. "I'm not *that* kind of doctor. Dr. Winschel wants to find out if we might find another reason for Maggie to stay a while with us, some way to absorb the cost of her stay. You see, we're a teaching hospital, which means we sometimes seek volunteers for special studies. While they are at the hospital, the expense of their stay is covered by the research program."

"No!" my mother said, abruptly standing up.

Dr. Berman ignored her and picked up the form that I'd filled out in the reception area. I'd written down everything I could remember about the night terrors—when they happened, how I felt before and after them, what kinds of accidents had happened to me. Her eyes moved hungrily over the words.

"I think you should give my offer more thought," she said slowly, her glance lifting to settle on my mother again. "Maggie has had some rough times with her terrors, and they don't seem to be leaving her on their own. In fact, they appear to be getting more violent. We've been studying these sorts of sleep disorders for quite a while and might be able to help her."

"You mean, other kids are like me?" I asked, sitting down at last.

"Others have terrors. But I've never come across anyone exactly like you, Maggie," she said. "In fact, your case is a very unusual one. I'd be interested in your staying with us for a few weeks."

She was no longer talking to my mother, only to me . . . as if *I* were the one who counted.

For the first time ever I felt as if I had something to say about my future. "My folks can't pay anything," I pointed out, just to be sure she understood.

"I know. As I've said, the cost of your stay will be covered by the research project, and your parents can stay in Hampton House." She glanced at my mother. "That's a boarding house attached to the hospital, where parents of long-term patients may stay without cost."

"No!" my mother repeated, her eyes grimly determined. "We aren't staying here."

"But Mom!" I cried, forgetting about my ribs. A jagged pain reminded me. "Maybe they could really help me!"

"I don't trust hospitals. They stick you with needles and cut you up, and for what?" she cried hysterically. "You'll be better off at home with me, where I can take

41

care of you. Terrible things happen in hospitals. Terrible things!"

My heart sank to the tips of my toes. For a moment, I'd dared to hope. But there was no reasoning with my mother when she flew off in one of her fits.

Dr. Berman came around her desk and squatted in front of my chair, placing her soft hands on my knees.

"Maggie, I think you're old enough to have a say in this. If you want medical help, just say so. Your parents should be willing to back you, since it will cost them nothing." She shot my mother a look of contempt. "And if they don't, I can call in a social services officer. I think they'll agree that your life will be in danger until your sleep disorder is cured. Your parents are jeopardizing your safety by refusing to let you stay where you can be helped."

"If you're thinking my mom and dad neglect me, they don't," I bit off. "They're good, kind people."

She patted my knees. "Possibly so. But to continue letting you suffer when participating in our study could help you . . . that's just not fair."

I glanced at my mother. There were tears in her eyes, and her hands were shaking as they clutched her purse to her plump stomach. "Please, sweetie. Let's just get out of here," she whimpered. "I'll take care of my little girl. These people don't even know you."

I took a deep breath, finding it awful to have to choose. "Mom, I know you try. I really do." I swallowed and swallowed again, searching for words. "But nothing we've done so far works. Maybe they can help me here. I want to get better!"

My mother didn't answer. She just stood there, getting paler by the second. My father sat stiffly in his chair, plucking lint from his pants leg.

"If you still refuse to grant your daughter permission to stay," Dr. Berman threatened, "I *will* go to the authorities."

My mother sniffled and searched through her purse for a Kleenex. "All right. But only for a few days . . . only

42

until they make sure she's not bleeding inside. You've got that long to stop her dreams, then we leave."

I stared at my mother. She'd always been the nervous type, but she was just about jumping out of her skin now. I wondered if what she'd said about hospitals was true. I wondered if I'd made a mistake by deciding to stay.

five

Opening my eyes, I lay very still as I studied the zillions of dots on the brilliant white acoustical tile above me. It took the dull throbbing in my shoulder and ribs to remind me I'd left my bedroom back in Winona and was in North Central Chicago Hospital. I still wasn't sure I'd made the right choice by staying. But I'd made it, so there was no point in worrying now.

At first Dr. Berman had wanted to put me in one of the sleep disorder rooms on the fifth floor. But she didn't have nursing personnel capable of dealing with sudden internal bleeding. She and Dr. Winschel decided I should stay in the adolescent surgery wing, just to be safe.

"We're giving you a private room," she explained, "to allow space for the polygraph machine and other special monitors. I'll hook you up whenever you lie down to sleep."

But I suspected there was another reason they wanted to keep me by myself. They weren't sure I could be trusted with another patient in the same room. They were afraid I might do something crazy.

I rolled my eyes toward the mirror on the back of the door and caught a glimpse of tiny electrodes attached to my face and head with something that looked like Silly Putty. Long, slender wires connected them to the two machines beside the bed. Carefully, I reached for the nurses' call button beside my pillow.

"You don't need that," a soft voice said.

44

I jerked around, surprised to find someone in the room. Dr. Berman pushed herself up out of a chair and set her clipboard on the night table beside my bed. She shut off a lamp with a red bulb that gave off a dim, eerie light just strong enough for her to see me in the dark as I slept and to make notes by.

"How long have you been here?" I asked. It was creepy, thinking about someone watching you sleep.

"All night," she said, then yawned. "I suppose you want me to pull your plugs so you can use the bathroom?"

"That would be nice," I commented dryly.

"No dreams last night," she said as she gently pulled away one electrode after another.

"No. But I kept waking myself up."

"I noticed. Is that how you avoid the night terrors?"

I nodded. "Force of habit. It usually works, unless I get super exhausted or lose my concentration at the wrong moment."

"Well, since we only have a limited time, I want you to do things during the day to get yourself really tired. Pack in the activities, including a good physical workout, and have fun. At night, just try to relax when you lie down. We *want* you to dream so we can see what's going on in your head, Maggie."

I looked at her pleadingly. "But it's so awful. I don't want to. . . ."

She was gazing at me with a kind expression. "I'm not going to let you die at the hands of your dream monster. And I won't let you hurt yourself while you're with me. Give in to the terrors just a few more times, and maybe we can stop them forever."

I sucked in a deep breath, focusing on her cool green eyes and nodded. "Okay. But how do I get exercise around a place like this?"

She laughed as she popped off the last sensor and stood back to give me a clear path to the toilet. "I don't think you'll have any trouble. There are lots of other kids in the teen ward who are well enough to be out of bed. They

45

spend most of the day in the lounge. We have a pool table, loads of board games, TV, a VCR and videos, and some exercise equipment—including two stationary bikes, a rowing machine, a rotary jogger, and a stepper."

"Really?" I was surprised. I'd imagined being confined to my little room for as long as I was in the hospital.

"Sure," she said. "And a volunteer wheels a book cart around, twice a day. She can sign out movies for you, or exercise videos. In your situation, I'll also let the nurses know they should encourage you to take brisk walks through the public areas of the hospital. But you'll have to stay inside the complex. No jogging through Grant Park."

I must have seen a picture of the park in one of the brochures Mrs. Simons had passed out at school before the field trip. The one I hadn't been able to take. My mind registered a flash of grassy space and a wide blue lake, sailboats, a ball field, and wooden swings hanging from thick chains that seemed to reach up into the sky.

"Okay," I said.

"If you want fresh air, there's a play lot on the roof for our younger patients—teeter-totter, a slide, and sandbox. That kind of thing. Get as much exercise as you can. We want you to sleep soundly."

She was talking through the bathroom door now, as I flushed the toilet and washed my hands and face. I looked in the mirror. Tiny cuts grazed the side of my right cheek where I'd rolled against the pavement. It was sore, a little puffy, and looked as if someone had scrubbed sandpaper across the flesh.

"Do you think it would hurt to put a little makeup over this?" I asked, stepping back into the room.

"Trying to look your best for the boys?" she teased, sounding more like Elly than a medical doctor.

I shrugged. "I'll just feel better, that's all."

She patted my back. "Go ahead. Do you need anything? Lipstick, eyeshadow, a heavier foundation?"

"No. I keep a small makeup bag in my purse," I said.

46

"Well, you have a busy and fun day." She wrote my name on a small card and slid it into a clear plastic holder with a pin on the back, making me a badge. "This will let you move around the hospital. Get to know some of the other kids while you're at it."

"I only have a few days," I reminded her, not wanting to make new friends, only to have to lose them so soon.

"Well," she said, with a conspiratorial wink, "there may be something we can do to keep you here longer."

I frowned, wondering what she meant as she gathered up her notes and rushed toward the door. It sounded sort of ghoulish. Who would want to be kept in a hospital longer than necessary?

"My extension is on that sheet of paper on the night stand, along with some instructions for you," she said, gesturing over her shoulder. "If you decide to take a nap, and when you get ready to sack out for the night, call me. Either I'll come to hook you up and sit with you, or I'll send one of my assistants."

"Okay."

I hadn't done much exploring the day before. I decided I'd try out my new badge and see what was up.

Since running up and down stairs would be good exercise, I avoided the elevators. After a half hour of roaming the hospital hallways and jogging from floor to floor, I came to two conclusions; one, North Central was enormous—practically a small city; two, I was lost.

I found a map in the visitors' lounge on the sixth floor and stopped to study it.

"Can I help you find some place?" a deep voice asked.

I spun around, expecting to see some thirty-year-old orderly. Instead, a boy about my age in a white lab coat stood looking down at me. *Way down.*

He was so tall I was eye level with the second button on his coat. I had to hitch up my neck at an uncomfortable angle to look into his face. He must have been closing in on seven feet, but he had the nicest dark brown eyes and a friendly smile.

"Hi," I said shakily. "I think I'm lost. I-I'm trying to get back to Adolescent Surgery."

His eyes lowered to the badge on my sweatshirt, and he frowned. "You're in the teen ward?"

"Yuh," I said, deciding I wouldn't try to explain about the nightmares and Dr. Berman. I didn't want him to think my deck was short a few cards. "Anything wrong with that?" I asked.

"No. Nothing." His glance dropped to the canvas straps that pinned my right arm across my chest, immobilizing my shoulder. "Broke your collarbone?"

I nodded.

"How'd you manage that? Fall off a bicycle? A car accident?"

"Sort of a car accident, but not really . . . Promise not to laugh?"

"Okay," he said solemnly.

"I fell out of my parents' car."

His long face broke into a grin.

"You promised!" I snapped accusingly.

"I didn't laugh, I smiled," he defended himself. "Besides, it's not every day a cute girl drops out of her car into my hospital."

"*Your* hospital?"

"Well," he chuckled, "I think of it that way. I spend so much time here, and I know everyone. They're like family."

"You're not some whiz-kid surgeon like Doogie Howser, are you?" I asked, studying him more closely. In addition to his lofty height, he had large hands— good for playing basketball. Winona could have used someone like him.

A couple of nurses stepped off the elevator, followed by a girl pushing a tiered cart loaded with books. They stared at us then moved off down the corridor. We must have looked funny standing together—him almost two feet taller than me.

"No," he said. "I wish I were a surgeon, though. I want to be one some day. Until I finish high school, I'm just a volunteer. Then I'll take my premed courses at the University of Chicago, if I can swing the scholarship I've been working on for the last two years."

"You sound like you've got your whole life mapped out."

He shrugged. "Not really, just some of the basic stuff. I don't want to do anything but be a doctor, so I might as well get started."

"I guess," I murmured. I wished my own life were smoother so I could make plans, too.

I glanced at his name tag—a blue one with his photo on it. Mine was yellow—no photo. "You're Bill Preston?" I murmured.

He laughed. "Yeah, sorry I didn't introduce myself." He peered at my tag again. "Margaret?"

I groaned. "Oh no! She put *that* on there?" I looked up at him, blushing. "Everyone calls me Maggie."

"Hi, Maggie," he said, holding out his hand.

I shook it, feeling sort of silly because the kids I knew never, ever shook hands. They held hands if they were dating, but they didn't shake like a couple of bankers.

But as soon as I grasped Bill's hand, I knew why he'd offered it. Because it wasn't a real shake, it was more like an invitation. His long fingers closed warmly around mine, and I felt them squeeze a message: *I like you. I want to see you again.*

My eyes opened wide, and I wet my lips, glad I'd put on the makeup. I slowly pulled my hand out of his, telling myself I really shouldn't let myself like anyone this fast. For all I knew, this guy hit on every female in the hospital!

"I'll walk you back to your room," he offered. "I have to go that way anyway, to escort a patient down to X ray. It's my last run before I have to leave for school."

49

"Okay," I agreed, figuring there was no harm in that.

We talked about the hospital, Chicago, and about Bill's home, which overlooked Lake Michigan. "It must be hard to afford a house on the water," I said.

He laughed. "Naw. My parents both work. Dad's an engineer for Techtronics, and Mom is a real estate agent. Besides, the house belonged to my grandparents. When they retired and moved to Florida, they sort of loaned the place to us, permanent."

When we at last reached my room on the third floor, I peeked inside. My breakfast tray was sitting on a special metal stand that stretched over the bed.

"Yummy," Bill said, rolling his eyes comically.

"You don't like the food here?" I asked.

"It's fine if you like bland," he commented. "I prefer Walker Brothers for breakfast. Great apple pancakes! And the Hard Rock Cafe's super for a thick, juicy burger."

"Well, I guess I'll have to make do since I don't have a choice." I lifted the aluminum lid from over the plate and sniffed at the evenly browned pancakes. They smelled a lot like warm cardboard. "Although," I added wistfully, "I've always wanted to see what the Hard Rock Cafe looks like."

He leaned down and whispered in my ear. "I'll spring you some time, and we can sneak over to West Ontario Street. It's less than a mile from here."

I stared at him, surprised he'd suggest such a thing. He must have known hospital rules. "I'm not supposed to leave the building."

"You're just here for observation, right?"

"Right," I agreed quickly. "I mean, there's nothing really wrong with me except this." I pointed to my shoulder with my good hand.

"Great!" he said enthusiastically. "Listen, there's a lot you're not *supposed* to do in life. Sometimes you have to take chances." His brown eyes darkened mysteriously, and he whispered. "Are you a chance taker, Maggie?"

"I . . . I don't know," I stammered, unsure of what he meant.

He smiled secretively, backing away toward the door. "People who take risks are more interesting."

Before I could ask him what he meant, he was gone.

"Strange," I muttered. But he was more than strange. Even with his towering height and stretched-out body, he was the coolest and best-looking guy who'd ever shown any interest in me.

Suddenly I felt like taking risks. I decided I wouldn't try to keep myself awake that night. I'd let the terrors find me. I'd sleep the sleep of the dead.

I ate the cardboard pancakes and missed Mrs. Reardon's homemade applesauce. As Bill had warned, the meal wasn't exactly packed with flavor. But everything was hot, and the thin slice of ham on the plate tasted okay after a night of trying to get comfortable on a taped-up shoulder.

Someone knocked on the door as I was polishing off my orange juice, and I looked up from my seat on the edge of the bed to see the girl who'd wheeled the book cart out of the elevator.

"Hi!" she said brightly.

"Hi!" I echoed back at her. I put down the empty glass. "I saw you on the sixth floor earlier this morning. You sure get around."

"I'll be up there again later today. I have to move fast," she said. "This place is pretty big, and I try to make two complete rounds of every ward, every day."

I smiled at her. She had a farm girl's face—round and creamy. She was a little heavier than she might be, but unlike my mother she didn't look at all flabby. There were muscles underneath the skin.

"You don't look old enough to be out of high school," I commented.

She laughed. "Who said I was?"

"No one. But if you're still in school—"

51

"I'm a senior," she explained. "I only need six credits to graduate, so I can sign up for a work-study program for the rest of the day. I spend all morning at the hospital, go to school for two classes in the afternoon, then come back here to finish my rounds between six and ten at night."

"Wow!" I breathed. "When do you have time to study?"

"For Phys Ed and Art?"

"*Those* are your two classes?"

She shrugged, flipping through a handful of index cards, putting them in order as she spoke. "I'd taken all my other requirements by the end of my junior year. I don't like gym and art, so I kept putting them off."

I shook my head in disbelief. "I wish I could do that."

"Why can't you?"

Because I never stayed in one place long enough to get a handle on my credits. "It's a long story," I muttered, pushing up off the bed and crossing the room to look out the window.

She tilted her head to one side and observed me. "Looks like you can move around okay. The nurse said you need lots of exercise. Why don't you walk around with me, and you can tell me your story."

"Okay," I agreed, checking out her badge. It said: VALERIE TUCKER. "Thanks, Valerie."

While we walked, I explained to her about all the moves we'd made, which had totally screwed up my class schedules and made some of my credits nontransferable. We knocked on doors and asked patients if they wanted a magazine, book, or video. They all knew Valerie, and she introduced me to everyone.

A few doors were closed and marked with plastic quarantine signs. We couldn't go into those rooms, and I told Valerie how sad I thought it was that people who were so sick couldn't even have the company of a good book.

"Oh, they can," she explained. "Contagious patients request books from their nurses. We keep a bunch of

52

paperbacks and magazines for that purpose. When they're finished with the book, it either goes home with them or it's destroyed."

"You mean, you never get the book back?"

"Right. You can't sterilize paper."

As we walked, Valerie gave me a running commentary on the various departments. "There's a new wing under construction. It will be eight floors, just like the main building," she said, pointing to a plastic curtain at the end of the hallway. A sign read: CONSTRUCTION AREA. NO ADMITTANCE. "That's where the entrance will be into this floor's extension. When all the floors are finished, there will be more bed space for many of the departments, plus a new cancer research unit."

"That's great," I said. "Maybe this is the hospital that will discover a cure."

"That would be wonderful, wouldn't it?" she agreed.

Before I knew it, the morning was nearly over, and I felt as if I knew the place inside out.

"I have to take off now," Valerie explained, as she locked the cart in a large storage closet lined with more books and tapes. "I hope your shoulder heals up real fast so you can go home. See you around."

Visiting hours were from noon to four that afternoon. Mom had one of her bad headaches and stayed at the guest house to rest. Dad spent most of the day hanging out in my room, bugging Dr. Winschel.

"How soon will you know about this internal stuff?" he demanded as soon as the doctor finished examining me.

"Another forty-eight hours . . . possibly," Winschel said. He looked seriously at my father. "You're in a rush to leave Chicago, Mr. Johnson?"

"I have a job lined up in Ohio," Dad said weakly. "I can't afford to lose it."

The doctor nodded. "Well, Maggie's a pretty big girl. Why don't you and your wife continue on, leaving us a phone number where you can be reached." He turned to me. "You wouldn't be afraid to stay by yourself, would you, Maggie?"

"Of course not."

"Are you sure?" my father asked hesitantly.

"Dr. Berman and Dr. Winschel are taking good care of me," I told him.

But it seemed as if there was something more that made me feel safe here. I'd felt a reassuring and strangely familiar sensation when I'd walked around the hospital that morning with Valerie. It was almost as if I'd been here before. But I knew I hadn't . . . unless it was in another life. Only I wasn't sure that I believed in stuff like that, coming back in another body after you died.

Of course, maybe it was just the people. They were all so friendly and kind.

"I'll be okay on my own," I repeated.

Dad stared thoughtfully at his palms. They were rough and callused from years of hard work in factory production lines and on warehouse loading docks.

"It's not a bad idea to get out of here," he muttered. Then he looked up at me sharply. "You're sure you don't want to come with us right now? I don't even have a phone number where we can be reached."

"I want to find out what's making me dream," I said softly, hoping he'd understand. "I can't stand it any more, Dad."

He winced and turned pale. "You've gone through a lot. . . . We all have . . ." Pulling in a deep breath, he stared at Winschel. "All right. I'll talk to her mother and see if I can convince her to come with me to Ohio tonight. Maggie can stay until you're sure she's okay."

"Good," Winschel said, looking pleased. He rested a hand on my good shoulder, as if to show my father he was taking over for him.

An hour later, Dad and I said our good-byes and I watched him step into an elevator. He looked so miserable, I wished I could do something to cheer him up.

I figured that getting well so he wouldn't have to chase me into the street in the middle of the night might be the best thing I could do for him.

I sighed and turned toward the patient lounge, wishing like crazy for something to take my mind off the beaten expression on my dad's face . . . and the night ahead with its too-familiar terrors.

six

Through the long glass wall I could see two boys bending over a pool table. They must have been just a year or two older than I. A girl who looked only twelve or thirteen was hanging out with them. One of her hands rested on an intravenous stand, which she wheeled around with her as she moved from one side of the table to the other, following the game.

The IV stand looked like a big silver coat rack, the kind waiting rooms in doctors' offices have when there's no closet. From it hung two plastic sacks of fluid that were connected by long, thin tubes to a needle taped into her arm. She didn't even seem to be aware of the needle, stand, or medicine trickling into her bloodstream as she jumped up and down excitedly whenever one of the boys knocked a ball into a pocket.

A few other kids lounged in armchairs, watching a video of Christian Slater's latest cop movie. For some reason I didn't feel as if I had as much in common with them as I had with Valerie, Bill, and the others who did volunteer work in the hospital. Which seemed a little odd, since I'd never done anything like that myself.

That got me thinking about Bill. I wondered if he'd be around tonight. He'd said he practically lived here.

I walked past the rec room windows to the elevator lobby. When the door opened, an orderly and a nurse stepped out. I stepped on and studied the panel of buttons before picking the lavender one, marked GERIATRICS.

When I stepped off it I was in another lobby the same size and shape as the one on my floor. But here, the walls were lined with pots of brightly colored flowers instead of rock posters.

I walked slowly down the hallway, noticing that this floor also had a lounge, but it was much smaller. There were only two people in it, sitting at a table, playing cards. They looked ancient.

Geriatrics, I remembered, meant the study of the problems and diseases of old people.

I walked toward the nurse's station. The two women behind the counter were frantically shuffling through files. They didn't even look up when I paused to ask if it was okay to look around.

One grabbed for the telephone. "It's not here, Doctor," she said in a panicky voice. "I *did* look everywhere! It's just not here!"

She threw the other nurse a hopeless look.

"Of course I understand how important it is," she continued. "But after all, the patient expired over a month ago. Central Records should have the complete file by now, or at least a duplicate and—"

She shut her mouth and gently massaged her temple as if she had Excedrin headache #35, then hung up the phone with a bang.

"Dr. Geringer's in one of his moods?" her friend commented.

"He's spitting mad," the telephone nurse moaned, "just because I can't find Mr. Murphy's floor chart. It's not supposed to be here any longer. Central Records should have it. I don't know why he's blaming me!" She was shouting now. I could hear her even as I walked farther down the hallway. "He says he's coming up here to look for it himself."

"Fat chance he'll find it," the other nurse said with a laugh.

I moved from door to door, glancing idly at the names on the cards, keeping an eye out for Bill. He'd mentioned that he liked working Geriatrics. It was possible he'd turn up here sometime during the evening.

"Well, don't just stand out there, Lucy!" a dry voice snorted. "Come in! Come in, girl!"

I looked around, wondering how I could have missed the other person standing in the hall. But no one else was around.

"You gonna hang outside that door all night?" the voice croaked.

Glancing at the card on the door, I read: MRS. ADELE KRANE.

Timidly, I poked my head inside the room. A white-haired, painfully thin old lady was propped up in the bed. She wore a pale pink cotton night dress with tiny flowers embroidered around the throat and cuffs. She sat proudly in the bed, as if it were a throne. In her lap rested a book, which supported a sheet of stationery.

"Are you talking to me?" I asked.

"Of course I am, do you see any other Lucys around?" the old lady demanded, shaking her pen at me.

Old people had always made me nervous, but there was something sweetly humorous about Mrs. Krane's confusion.

"My name is Maggie," I said gently, "but I'll still come in if you'd like company."

The old woman peered into my face. "I shouldn't be alone, you know," she said.

"Why is that?"

"What are you—blind? I'm old!"

I giggled. "Well, I can sort of see that . . . but you're not *too* old," I added quickly, not wanting to be rude.

"I'm ninety-one years of age," Mrs. Krane stated, her voice breaking on a rattly cough that sounded as if she was just getting over a bad cold. "That's pretty damn old, Lucy."

I sighed and decided not to quibble about my name. "So," I said, pulling a chair up alongside the bed, "how are you feeling today?"

"Pretty good." Mrs. Krane smiled sunnily. "I've been very busy, of course, but that's good for the soul."

"Busy?"

"Writing to all of my friends. I've finished six letters today." She tapped the pen on the stationery box near her left hip and winked at me. "My letters have very important information. But it's a secret."

I thought she was adorable with her sparkling blue eyes, white hair that shone like an angel's halo, and lovely smile. She might be daffy, but I decided she'd be fun to sit and talk with. We chatted for almost two hours before one of the nurses poked her head in and looked surprised to see me there.

"You have a guest, Mrs. K! How nice!"

"This is my daughter Lucy," Mrs. Krane said with a grand flourish of her arm.

The nurse winked at me, as if to let me know she was playing along with the joke. "So very nice to meet you, Lucy."

Laughing, I shook the nurse's hand. To be Mrs. Krane's daughter, I'd have to be at least fifty years old.

"My daughter came all the way from Pittsburgh to see me," Mrs. Krane explained solemnly. "She is a very important woman who runs her own business."

"Oh well, it *is* nice that you were able to make the trip," the nurse said with a straight face.

"Is your cousin Frank here yet?" Mrs. Krane asked, looking at me.

I shot a questioning look at the nurse, who subtly shook her head.

"No," I answered. "He couldn't come today."

Mrs. Krane looked disappointed. "He lives right here in Chicago, you know. And he's come only once to see me." Her eyes sparked with anger as she hissed, "He wants my money when I kick off, but he won't bother visiting with an old woman to get it!"

"Now, now, Mrs K," the nurse soothed her. "Don't

59

upset yourself about him. See? Lucy's here. That's what's important."

The old woman smiled softly. "Yes, now that you're here, dear Lucy, I don't need to send these letters." A sly look crossed her face. "But maybe I should anyway, just for insurance, don't you see?"

The nurse shot me a glance that said, *I'll explain this later.*

Then she said aloud, "It's getting kind of late. Maybe you'd better get some sleep, Mrs. K. A nasty bout with pneumonia takes a lot out of a woman your age."

"All right," the old woman said agreeably. "If you'll mail my letters."

The nurse took them from her. "They'll go out first thing tomorrow morning," she promised, tucking them into the pocket of her uniform.

"Good. That's very good," murmured Mrs. Krane, her eyes already looking heavy.

The nurse turned to leave, and I started to follow her.

"Wait, Lucy! Just a word alone with you?" Mrs. Krane called out.

I glanced at the nurse, who nodded, and I walked back to the bed. When the old woman beckoned me down with a crooked finger, I bent close to her wrinkled face.

"I have a secret," she murmured. "The letters will tell my friends the truth, but you should know, too . . . in case something happens."

I grinned. She was like a little kid, needing reassurance that everything would be okay before allowing Mom to turn off the light for the night. I patted her shoulder. "Nothing's going to hap—"

The old woman's hand snapped up, clutching the front of my shirt and dragged me down with surprising strength to within an inch of her hot breath.

"They are trying to kill me!" she rasped out.

I gulped down a bubble of fear. She was a lot stronger than she looked.

60

"No one's trying to kill you," I choked out, struggling to escape the woman's bony grip.

"They are!" she screamed. "They will *do* it, just like they killed the others—"

"Mrs. Krane!" a voice boomed from the doorway.

A man in surgeon's garb loomed in the doorway. His brows were so bushy they formed a low, dark ridge over his eyes. His hair, raggedly trimmed and graying around the temples, was brushed back haphazardly. His body was rigid with anger.

"Who are you?" he demanded, stepping forward and glaring at me.

"Why, Doctor, don't you recognize Lucy, my dear daughter? Remember, I showed you her picture."

I pointed shakily at my badge. "I . . . I'm from Adolescent Surgery. I just stopped in to visit with—"

"What are you doing on this floor?"

He kept asking questions but didn't give me a chance to explain. Even though I hadn't done anything wrong, I got a nervous feeling in the pit of my stomach.

I tried again. "I was just taking a walk, when Mrs. Krane called me in and I—"

"Get out of here!" the man growled. He stood aside and jerked his head toward the doorway.

He wasn't a big man, but his anger was impressive.

I slipped timidly past him into the hall. At the desk, one of the nurses was scurrying around like a little mouse on a treadmill.

That must have been Dr. Geringer, I thought, sorry I'd crossed his path.

I practically broke into a run, ignoring Dr. Winschel's warning to not jar my injured ribs. But when I reached the elevator lobby, the nurse who'd stepped into Mrs. Krane's room was waiting for an elevator.

She forced a smile. "I'm sorry you got yelled at. He's really an excellent surgeon, he just has these fits of temper sometimes and no one's safe."

"Did I do something wrong?" I asked.

61

"Technically, maybe. People aren't really supposed to wander the halls. Ambulatory patients are welcome anywhere in their own ward or in the public areas, like the cafeteria or lounges. But the private rooms of other wards are supposed to be off-limits."

"I didn't know," I murmured. "Sorry. Dr. Berman said I should get lots of exercise."

The elevator doors eased open. No one was inside, and the nurse stepped on. I followed her.

"Normally, if a geriatric patient gets a visitor, we're thrilled," she continued. "Some have no families to speak of. They get terribly lonely, and the company does them good."

I nodded, thinking again about what Mrs. Krane had been saying at the moment Dr. Geringer showed up.

The elevator stopped, and the nurse stepped out. It wasn't my floor, but I followed her anyway, wanting to ask her about Mrs. Krane's fears. Before I could say anything, though, she stepped over to a trash bin, took the letters out of her pocket, and tossed them in.

"Hey!" I shouted. "Why did you do that?"

The nurse shook her head sadly. "It won't do any good to mail them."

"Why not?"

"Those people all died years ago," she explained. "Mrs. Krane remembers family and friends from her past. She forgets she went to their funerals."

I swallowed. "How sad . . ." Then I remembered her *secret*. "Listen, she said something as I was leaving the room, something Dr. Geringer interrupted."

"What was that?"

"She said that someone is trying to kill her, that there have been others in this hospital who'd been murdered, and that she was next."

The nurse frowned. "Poor dear, I'll bet she believes every word of it, too."

"You mean, all this talk about murders and killing people . . . that's something she imagines, too?"

"Not all of it, I suppose." She glanced at her watch as if she were worried about missing an appointment. "A lot of our patients are very upset whenever anyone in the ward expires. They sometimes get to know one another quite well. Unfortunately, in the last three months, we've lost several patients."

"So you think she's just overreacting to natural deaths?"

"Of course. Just because people are old doesn't mean that death isn't still scary. And she's recovering from a bad case of pneumonia. I'm sure she's feeling very vulnerable."

Still, I couldn't get Mrs. Krane's desperate words out of my mind.

"But she was going to name someone . . . someone she said was responsible for killing them."

The nurse shook her head and gazed solemnly at me. "You've heard of Alzheimer's disease, haven't you, Maggie?"

I nodded.

"Mrs. K. often doesn't know what she's saying. Oh sure, she has her lucid moments, but they come and go so quickly. She gets awfully confused. You saw how she mistook you for her daughter."

My heart lifted. "Her daughter Lucy! Maybe we could get her to come and—"

The expression on the nurse's face brought me to a stop.

"What?" I asked.

"Lucy died two years ago at the age of sixty-eight. Mrs. Krane was too feeble to make it to the funeral in Pittsburgh, but she was told of Lucy's death."

"Oh," I murmured.

On my way back to the third floor, I spotted a lanky figure in a lab coat. Bill Preston. A pleasant shiver ran up my spine, and I felt a surge of energy.

I ran down the hall toward him. He turned around a second before I reached him.

"Hi there!" he said, smiling. "I stopped by your room, but the duty nurse said she hadn't seen you in a couple of hours."

"I was just walking around, visiting patients," I said. "And catching hell from one of the doctors."

He laughed. "That's happened to me plenty of times. They act like they own the place. Which one got you?"

"Geringer."

He groaned and rolled his eyes. "You poor kid. He's a mean one. I try to steer clear of him."

"I wasn't doing anything wrong, just visiting this sweet little old lady. She's my newest friend."

I don't know when I'd started thinking of Mrs. Krane as my friend. We'd only spent a few hours together. But I'd never had a grandmother, and she had seemed to me the perfect grandma type—even if she was old enough to be my great or great-great grandmother.

"What's her name?" he asked.

"Adele Krane."

A smile tugged at his lips. "What stories has she been telling *you*?"

"That someone wants to kill her."

I expected him to laugh out loud, but he didn't. After a minute, he said softly, "Man, these old folks come up with some beauties, don't they!"

"She believes it, I could tell. That's what's so sad."

"Yeah, well—" he wiped a drop of sweat from his forehead with the knuckles of one hand "—that's why you can't believe most of what they tell you. Sometimes they lose all sense of reality."

"I know," I murmured. "Still, Mrs. K is nice and Geringer shouldn't have run me off the way he did. He could have been polite and asked me to leave so she could get some rest."

"That's what I would have done," Bill said. "Don't worry about him. Come on, let's go find something to do in the lounge. It's only eight-thirty, and I'm officially off-duty now."

We looked through all the board games and found a set of Tri-Ominoes. I hadn't played in years. Before long there was a crowd of kids around us—some on crutches, others pushing around their IV stands—all arguing about the rules and helping us spot places to play the little plastic triangles.

At ten o'clock the rec room closed, and the patients drifted off to their own rooms. Hospital rules.

"I gotta go anyway," Bill said after he'd walked me back to my room. "School tomorrow."

"Oh," I said, a little disappointed.

I'd sort of hoped he'd hang out with me a couple more hours. Sometimes I forgot that other people slept longer than three hours a night. Then I remembered that I'd promised Dr. Berman I'd welcome the night terrors.

I closed my eyes for a moment as a tremor of fear crept through my bones. I quickly opened them.

"Will you be around tomorrow?" I asked softly.

"Count on it," Bill said, smiling. He turned to leave, then spun back and, folding his long body down, kissed me quickly on the cheek. "Sweet dreams!"

For a long time I stood in the middle of my room, touching my face where his lips had brushed. I suddenly felt braver than I'd ever felt before. I crossed to the phone and punched in Dr. Berman's extension.

She answered almost immediately.

"I'm ready to go to sleep," I said.

seven

I am walking through the same corridors I've walked at night since I was very, very young. People smile pleasantly at me and say hello, but there is something different about the dream this time.

This time I know where I am. There is no doubt in my mind that this isn't a factory or a school or a business complex. I am in North Central Chicago Hospital. All the details feel right—the rooms off of the main corridor, the intersecting passages leading off to different departments and wards, the smell of disinfectant and medicines. . . .

And there is something else I'm suddenly sure of— I'm not fifteen years old. The people who pass by are all looking down at me, as if I've shrunken. Even the shortest adults have to drop their glance to meet my eyes as we pass. And when they say, "Why, hello there! How are you today?" they say it in that cutesy way I talk to real little kids I baby-sit.

When I take a step, it doesn't take me far, because my legs must be terribly short. I look around for a mirror, wanting to see what I look like, but there are none along the mint green walls.

At last the corridor narrows and darkens, snaking away from me treacherously. I follow it, although the fear is already rising in my stomach and tightening my chest so that I have trouble breathing. Then I hear her steps . . . running . . . running after me.

I'm aware that I'm not supposed to resist the night terror. I tell myself that I must open myself fully to its powers, though I can't remember why. I turn to face the wild woman, and she's still a couple of hundred feet away. But if I don't take off, she'll catch up with me in seconds, for she's running as hard as she can, her mouth contorted into an ugly shape as she gulps down air, her arms pumping at her sides like an Olympic athlete.

Something inside of me whispers, "She's coming for me. Just wait . . . wait . . . let her catch up. . . ."

But a force outside of me jerks me away, and suddenly my feet are churning, skimming over the floor, and the walls fly past as I tear around a corner and into a shaft. . . . Then I'm falling down . . . down . . . down.

The voice behind us . . . us? Why do I think 'us'? The voice behind me is hysterical with fury. The woman shrieks, "Stop, stop! I'll kill you, stop!"

I know the voice, and I know she means it. If she catches us—there I go again—if she catches me, she'll stab me with her knife. I can imagine, as if in a horror movie, her blade plunging into my flesh, then withdrawing— blood spurting from a gaping wound in my side as I collapse, holding my organs inside with my hands as I cry out in agony.

"Maggie. Maggie! Wake up, honey. . . ."

I scream, wanting to be left alone to die in peace. I know that if I open my eyes, she will be there with her bloody knife, taunting me . . . glorying in my death throes.

"Maggie, it's me . . . Dr. Berman. It's all right now, wake up. We have work to do."

At the word *work*, my mind shifted gears. I opened my eyes and stared at a woman in a coral pink sweater, matching slacks, and pearls.

"Dr. Berman!" I gasped. "Oh, God . . . it was terrible. She was there, chasing me, and I wanted to stop and face her but something pulled me on and I almost got away, but . . ."

"Sit down, Maggie!" she instructed me firmly, one hand pressing down on my shoulder, the other clamped around my left wrist. She was already taking my pulse, even as she eased me down onto a chair.

"Where are we?" I asked, my voice cracking, my throat as dry as dead leaves.

I stared around the unfamiliar room. We were only a few feet from one of the walls where the construction crews had broken through to add the new wing. An icy draft slipped through the plastic-curtained opening.

"You tore off the electrodes and ran out of your room," Dr. Berman explained. "We're on the first floor, in the administrative offices. No one's here; they work only during the day."

I nodded, taking in details of the business office—a lot of computers and telephones, a fax machine in one corner, copier in another. The fluorescent lights overhead were on; probably Dr. Berman had thrown the switch as she ran in after me.

"How did I get here?" I gasped, wiping sweat from my upper lip with the back of my hand.

"The personnel stairs. Have you been taking them to get around on your walks?"

"I guess so," I said, trembling all over. "I mean . . . no, I don't think so." I squeezed my eyes shut, trying to remember. "I took the elevator when I was making rounds with Valerie. When I was on my own I used some stairs, but they were the ones open to the public."

She nodded, her fingers finally releasing my wrist. Pulling a second wheeled typing chair up beside mine, she took a notebook and pen from her slacks pocket and sat down. "I know you'd be more comfortable in your own room, but I want to ask you some questions right away, while your memory is freshest. Okay?"

"Sure," I said. "I just can't stop shaking. She was so close, and it was so real. I could see the blood when she stabbed me. I could feel the knife go in."

"Then, the woman did catch you this time?" she asked, writing furiously in a spiky shorthand.

"No-o-o-o," I said slowly, mentally sorting through the scenes that were already beginning to fade. "I knew she was very close, then we were falling through a deep tunnel, or maybe it was down a stairwell—"

"You were adding the reality of your running through the hospital and down the stairs to your dream story . . . interesting," she murmured, her hand moving rapidly across the page.

"I guess I was," I agreed. "Anyway, then the vision stopped, but I could imagine what would happen next. What it would be like if she caught me and if she cut me. It was just as real as the night terror."

"But it sounds as if there's an important difference. You shifted out of a dream you couldn't control to one where you could add your own details. You were imagining the logical consequences of her attack, if she caught up with you."

"I guess," I said doubtfully.

"Maggie, were you able to see anything more specific in the setting of the night terror this time?"

"Yes," I said excitedly. "Yes, I was in this hospital."

She nodded without commenting, but kept on writing.

"It's funny, until now I've never had a sense of the place being one in particular. I've never recognized it."

"Could be your surroundings have changed so dramatically in the last two days you've included them in your dream."

I shrugged. "Maybe." But somehow it seemed to be more than that. "There was one other thing. . . ."

"Yes?"

"I wasn't me, or at least I wasn't me *now*."

She frowned at that. "What do you mean?"

"I was very little. People in the beginning of the dream were looking down at me, as if I was very short. They were being nice to me—saying hi, and stuff like that—but not as if I was fifteen. More like I was a little kid."

Her eyes lit up, and she wrote even faster. "Good. This is very good, Maggie."

"What's good about it?"

"Well, we know that things that happen early in our childhood often make powerful impressions on the rest of our lives. It's possible that something traumatic happened when you were very young, and that triggered the night terrors. Once begun, they'll stay with you until you confront their source."

I took a deep breath and stared at her, blood pounding in my forehead. "Nothing really awful has ever happened to me. I mean, I broke my arm once and another time I got cut up pretty bad, but those were both accidents that happened after the terrors started."

"When?" she asked, looking intently into my eyes. "When exactly did they happen?"

"Well, I broke my arm when I was ten years old. I ran into the street and a passing car. I think I was about seven when I crashed through the bedroom window."

"So whatever prompted your terrors must have happened before you were seven," she murmured, writing the number seven very big on the page. "How far back do you remember, Maggie?"

"I don't know. I remember playing dolls with some friends. I think I was in first grade." I laughed, remembering a stupid argument I'd had with one of the little girls. Her name had been Cindy Smith. "I gave a friend my favorite doll, as a going-away present. I was the one moving. Then I changed my mind and wanted it back. She wouldn't give it to me. I cried for days."

"Did you eventually get your doll back from her?"

I clenched my teeth, wishing my head would stop hurting so I could think clearly. "No, I don't think I did. I think we moved before we could settle the fight."

"That would have been pretty disturbing, but probably not enough to trigger a lifelong series of night terrors.

Try to think back even earlier," she encouraged.

"I can't," I said, throwing up my hands. "That's it . . . everything else is hazy."

"What about old family pictures? They might jog your memory."

"We don't have many. Dad's not big on taking snapshots."

"School photographs?"

"You know how it is when you move around a lot. Stuff like that just seems to disappear."

Dr. Berman drew a deep breath and nodded. "All right, is there anything more?"

"No," I said regretfully, "that's all I can think of now." I looked at her, scrunching up her nose and glaring down at her notes. It was obvious her mind was racing at megaspeed. "What about you?" I asked. "Do you know anything more about me than before?"

"Yes-s-s-s," she said slowly with a gentle smile, "although I'm not sure how it will solve the mystery of Maggie."

"Tell me."

"Well, as I'd suspected, you aren't having classic night terrors. You're mixing nightmares and terrors— two completely different problems. In night terrors, the person usually has no memory of the dream. She wakes suddenly with a vague sense of danger, but can't tell where it's come from. She'll often leap up from the bed and sometimes run through the house, not waking even if someone shakes her or throws cold water on her. She can't remember how she got from her bed to wherever she ends up."

I nodded, concentrating bard on her words.

She continued. "Night terrors happen during a partial awakening state. Somewhere between deep sleep and being fully alert and aware of your surroundings. For some reason, the brain doesn't kick all the way into gear. On the other hand, nightmares are in REM. You dream and remember your dreams, but you can't get

71

up and move around while they're happening. There's a kind of paralysis built in to REM, probably nature's way of protecting us from hurting ourselves."

"Does this mean I'm going crazy?" I asked weakly.

She laughed and hugged me. "Not at all! You're just working out some problem in your mind. Something that doesn't compute, that you can't make sense of in your waking time."

"If I remember back far enough, will we find the reason?"

"There's a good chance," she said. She looked with concern at me. "Are you tired now? Can you sleep?"

"Yeah. I think so."

"Good," she said, standing up and turning toward the door. She grasped my hand to bring me along with her.

"*No!*" I screamed, cringing from her touch and pulling away.

She stared at me, and I stared back at her, shocked at the way I'd reacted to her. A minute ago, she'd been hugging me, and I'd trusted her—at least, I thought I trusted her.

"Why did you do that, Maggie?" Her voice was low, and her eyes narrowed suspiciously, studying me. "You know I wouldn't hurt you."

"I know, of course I know," I said quickly. But I was shaking all over. "I'm sorry, it just came out."

She bent closer to me and whispered, "Think, Maggie. Think of the feelings that made you pull away from me. What were you afraid of?"

The shaking became uncontrollable. "Oh geez," I breathed. "It was the dream."

"What about it?" she asked tightly.

"A couple of times during the terror, I thought *we* instead of *I*. . . ." I shook my head, knowing I must sound like I'd totally flipped out. "This is really confusing, I'm sorry. It was as if I was no longer alone when I ran away from the woman. There was someone with me. When I stopped running and looked back at the crazy woman

72

chasing me, the person grabbed my hand and forced me to run."

"Someone was there helping you?" she asked.

"I . . . I guess so."

"Was this person there the other times you dreamed?"

I thought for a moment, at first unsure. "Yes," I said at last. "I think he or she was there all along, but I didn't realize it before."

She carefully put her arm around me. "Good, it's coming back to you. Tomorrow night you may remember more. At least now you know you weren't alone in your night terror. Someone was there to help you."

I nodded slowly. I wanted to believe her but somehow the idea felt all wrong.

"If I knew who the person was, who was trying to help me . . . maybe we could figure out the rest of the terror," I said.

"Possibly."

"But the dream ends too soon. I never get to see the other person."

Dr. Berman started walking, and this time I followed her willingly toward the elevator. "I'll tell you a secret," she said. "You have the power to manipulate your dreams, to make them longer or change what happens in them."

I shivered. "I never thought I'd want to make them *longer*."

"Look at it as a scientific experiment. Next time you dream, make yourself stop running. Then tell your dream body to turn around and face the wild woman. Ask her what she wants from you."

"Are you kidding?" I gasped. "She wants to *kill* me. She'll laugh in my face, then stab me!"

"Maybe not. Maybe she'll just tell you why she's been chasing you all these years."

"Really?"

Dr. Berman smiled encouragingly as we stopped in front of the elevator doors. "Really. It's worth a try, don't you think?"

73

I wasn't sure. "But what if the dream ends before I can ask her or she can answer? How do I make the dream longer, like you said I could?"

"You dream spin," she said.

"Huh?"

"You tell your dream self to hold out her arms, and spin around and around. It might sound silly, but we've found that patients who can dream spin are able to extend a dream or force it into another scene. I've done it myself."

"I don't know." I swallowed the lump of fear clogging my throat. "It sounds strange. I want the terrors to stop and go away, not get longer or worse."

Dr. Berman turned me to face her, ignoring the open elevator doors waiting for us. "They won't stop until you find their cause . . . the reason the terrors started in the first place. You have to face that, Maggie."

I closed my eyes tightly and tried to talk in a normal voice, but the words sounded raspy. "I just don't know how much more I can take."

"Be strong," she said. "You can do it."

I nodded, hoping she was right.

eight

After Dr. Berman walked me back to my room, I lay for a long time in the hospital bed, wanting to sleep while she watched over me. I couldn't.

We played cards for an hour, less to amuse me than to keep her awake. I could tell she was exhausted and wanted to go home to bed herself. But she felt she shouldn't leave me, even though I told her at 3:00 A.M. that it was safe for me to nap for a few hours without her there.

At last she gave instructions to one of the floor nurses to check on me every half hour, then she went home. I lay back on my pillow, starving for even a few hours of dreamless sleep. I closed my eyes.

I woke up to find the sun out. I couldn't remember falling asleep. My eyes burned, like most mornings, but I knew I shouldn't try to sleep any longer. That would be dangerous.

Besides, I was restless. What I'd discovered in last night's terror made me want to learn more.

The first thing I saw when I sat up in bed was a huge silvery rainbow floating over the foot of my bed. I grinned at the bouquet of balloons.

"Looks like you have a secret admirer," a voice remarked from the doorway.

It was Valerie. She was wearing her pink cotton candy-striper smock over white leggings. She wheeled her cart into the room.

75

"Someone special from home?" she asked.

"I don't know," I said honestly. I thought of Mom and Dad first, then immediately decided the balloons couldn't have come from them. With the cost of the move, they didn't have money to blow on anything as impractical as balloons.

I reached up to pull the bunch down closer to me. There were at least a dozen of them. One with roses on it said "You're Special!" Another was in the shape of a teddy bear hugging a heart. The message on a third read "Beep! Beep! Hurry up and get well!" It was decorated with a Road Runner cartoon character on one side and Wile E. Coyote on the back.

"They must be from my friend back home," I said, thinking of Elly.

But how had she found out about my accident? I doubted that my parents would have called her or anyone else back in Winona. What could they tell people except the embarrassing truth? I'd thrown myself out of a speeding car!

"There's a card tied to one of the ribbons," Valerie pointed out.

I pulled the pink satin strand toward me and opened the tiny envelope. "*Hope you're feeling better soon . . . but not too soon,*" I read silently. Why would anyone say that? I turned over the card, looking for a signature. "*I want you to hang around here for a while,*" the writing continued. "*Hugs and kisses, Bill!*"

I felt as if I'd burst with happiness. "They're from Bill Preston. Isn't that sweet?"

Valerie let out a little huffing noise. "You've got to be kidding!"

Something about her tone seemed odd. "No. Why should I be?"

She shrugged. "He's always so serious, so wrapped up in school and medicine and all. . . . I don't think he even dates."

"Really?" I asked, surprised. He was really good looking, although in a different sort of way. And he'd seemed nice.

Valerie started reorganizing the top shelf of her book cart. "Don't get me wrong. I think he likes girls. At least he's always friendly and polite to me and the other girls at school. It's just that he seems to be on a real rigid schedule—school, homework, the hospital, back to school again. . . . I figure girls just don't have a place in his life."

I smiled, feeling very special . . . just like the balloon said. "Oh," I murmured happily.

A warm feeling stayed inside of me all day. Every time I looked at the balloons, I thought about Bill and how sweet he was to try to cheer me up. I wondered if he liked me as a friend, or if he'd thought about getting . . . well, romantic. I remembered his kiss. *Romantic*, I thought. *Definitely romantic*.

I killed time during the morning, playing Scrabble and Hearts with other patients in the lounge. One girl had been in a bad car accident and was in traction after she'd had a steel pin surgically implanted in her leg. A nurse wheeled her, bed and all, into the lounge, and two of the other girls who were well enough to be up walking around brought her books to read and a Game Boy to play with.

Other kids never came out of their rooms, but a nurse told me that most would eventually be able to join us. Some had just had surgery. Others were taking medications that made them too sleepy to get out of bed safely or enjoy company.

After lunch I decided to walk up to Mrs. Krane's room. It was visiting hours, so I figured I couldn't get into trouble. When I walked in, she was asleep.

For a moment I stood in the doorway, watching her and feeling a little disappointed that she wasn't awake. Her cheeks were a healthy, rosy shade, and her chest rose and fell in slow, even puffs. She sounded as if the pneumonia had eased up; there was no rattling in her breath, no effort in her breathing. I smiled, glad that she was going to get

77

better. Before long, she'd probably be going home.

I turned to leave the room but caught a glimpse of an envelope, peeking out from beneath the sheets and her crossed hands. Curious, I moved closer to her. She'd probably been writing letters to her dead friends again.

I smiled sadly. "I'll mail it for you," I whispered, remembering how the nurse had reassured her, then disposed of the hopeless messages. It would be upsetting for her if she really mailed them and the Post Office returned them with an Addressee Unknown stamp.

I slipped the mauve paper rectangle out from under her wrinkled, blue-veined hands and turned it over so that I could read the writing. There was no address, only the name: Lucy.

"Oh, no," I sighed.

Well, it didn't matter that there was no address since it was headed for the trash can anyway.

Or . . . maybe she'd meant the note for me. On second thought, she probably had intended to give it to me, since she hadn't addressed it. I slipped the letter into my jeans pocket and walked out of the room.

Looking down the hall, I could see the nurses' station. A man in a trim charcoal gray business suit stood reading a chart, a stethoscope looped around his neck. He looked familiar—something about the way he stood with one foot slightly in front of the other, his head bowed over the patient's chart. Then I realized who it was.....

Geringer.

I whipped around abruptly, hoping to locate the back stairs Dr. Berman had mentioned, but he must have spotted me.

"Hey, you!" he shouted. "What are you doing back on this floor?"

I started running. I didn't know why he should scare me so much, but he did. His gruff voice felt as if it were slicing through me. The anger seemed way out of proportion to my transgression if it was a crime to visit another floor during visiting hours.

I tore down the hall and around a corner, searching for an Exit sign, then spotted the glowing red letters above and to my right. My ribs hurt; the running motion was jerking on the tape, making the bones throb and my skin pinch. I dived for the exit but forgot about my bad shoulder and whacked it against the door while trying to push it open.

"Ah!" I screamed, flinching as I tumbled into the stairwell.

My foot slipped off the threshold, and I was suddenly pitching forward, over a long flight of cement stairs. A big hand shot out and grabbed my shirt, wrenching me back onto the landing.

"What do you think you're doing?" Geringer demanded, giving me a firm shake before releasing me.

I glared at him defiantly. "I went to see my friend, Mrs. Krane. It's visiting hours, and I have permission to leave my floor."

"You don't have Mrs. Krane's doctor's permission to visit her," he said. "I'm her doctor."

Something wicked inside of me prodded me to give him a smart-mouthed comeback. "Just the man I wanted to see. May I visit Mrs. Krane?"

He blinked at me, dark eyes glittering beneath dense brows. His glare took in my taped shoulder, then the yellow badge. "Why were you admitted to this hospital? We don't hospitalize broken collarbones."

"Internal injuries," I said. "I'm being observed."

He scowled. "How can anyone observe you if you're running all over the place?"

"I'm supposed to get exercise. Helps me sleep at night." I took a deep breath for courage and glared back at him. "You didn't answer me. Can I visit Mrs. Krane during regular visiting hours?"

He stared at me as if he wasn't used to people standing up to him when he ordered them around. But he still didn't answer.

I tried again. "I said—"

"I heard what you said," he barked. "I don't want you back on this floor, for any reason."

"Why not? Mrs. Krane is lonely."

"You'll go back to your ward and stay there!" he shouted.

The louder he yelled, the more stubborn I felt. "My doctor says I can walk around."

His eyes turned brittle with frustration. "Who is your doctor?"

"Dr. Berman," I said before I could stop myself. I chewed my bottom lip, watching his expression turn thoughtful. I realized, too late, that I should have told him it was Winschel.

"Berman," he repeated, "but she has nothing to do with orthopedic surgery or——" He broke off, his eyes narrowing. "You're one of her sleep disorder patients?"

"Yes," I admitted.

"What exactly is she treating you for?" he asked.

"I have bad dreams, that's all." I was anxious to get away from him now. I didn't like the way he was looking at me, with suspicion and interest at the same time. "I should go now," I said.

"Wait." His hand clutched my good arm, squeezing so hard that it hurt. "How long have you been here? How long have you been a patient at this hospital?"

"Two days," I said quickly. "Let me go!"

"Two days? That's all?"

"That's all," I said, pulling out of his grip. I backed away.

He took a threatening step toward me. "Then you've only known Mrs. Krane that long?"

"Right." I noticed that the nurses at their station were watching us now.

He must have followed my glance, for he took two steps away from me as if he were afraid they'd see something he didn't want them to see.

Strangely, his nervousness made me braver. "Is Mrs. Krane going to be all right?" I asked.

80

"Mrs. Krane?" he repeated, distracted. "Sure, she'll be going home tomorrow."

I nodded. "Good. She seems like a nice lady." Turning around, I quickly walked toward the elevator. I felt a dangerous prickly sensation. I knew Geringer was watching me.

I banged the down arrow with my fist. The door slid open, and I stepped on.

I was almost back to my room before I'd caught my breath and my heart quit thudding in my chest. I swung the door shut behind me.

I didn't know why Geringer should affect me the way he did. I was scared of him, but at the same time as curious about him as he seemed to be about me. I wanted to find out why he'd gone bananas when I'd tried to talk with one of his patients.

What was he afraid of? And why did he always act so intense—picking on the nurses when they couldn't find some old chart and going off the deep end just because a kid-patient was wandering around the building? Maybe he was just a—

"Jerk," I muttered.

I tore open the flap of Mrs. Krane's envelope and, plunking down on the bed, pulled out a pretty mauve sheet of stationery. It was dated today.

DEAR LUCY,

Please come back to see me as soon as you can. I fear I may never return to my own dear home. I was wrong when I wrote before and said that man was a harmless fool. He's dangerous! If someone doesn't stop him, he will kill me just as he killed the others. I don't understand why he hurt them, when it was me he was after. There must be no end to his evil. Please help me!

YOUR LOVING MOTHER,
ADELE KRANE

81

I sat on my bed, unable to pull any air into my lungs. The handwriting was weak and scratchy, but the meaning of the words was clear enough. Or were they simply the ramblings of a lonely and confused old lady?

"What's that?" a voice asked.

I hastily folded the sheet and twisted around to face the door. "Oh, hi, Bill!" I shrugged. "Nothing, just a note from a friend. You know, 'Heard you got banged up. Hope you get better.' That sort of thing."

I didn't understand why I was fibbing to him, but my brain had started racing and spitting out crazy warnings as soon as he'd stepped in the room. *He,* the note had said, *he* was dangerous. Mrs. Krane had obviously meant someone here at the hospital, or at least someone who had access to the place. *Until I can talk to her, I'd better not trust anyone,* I thought.

I stuffed her letter under my pillow and stood up.

"Thanks for the great balloons," I said.

He grinned. "Like them?"

"Yeah. They were the first thing I saw when I woke up this morning."

He nodded, looking pleased. "The gift shop has a lot to choose from. They deliver for free."

"Maybe Mrs. Krane would like a bunch," I thought out loud.

"I heard she was going home tomorrow," he said. "Better order them soon if you're going to at all."

But Mrs. Krane believed she'd never see her home again, I thought sadly. "How sick is she?" I asked. "I mean, is she super senile? Does she imagine a lot of things?"

"She gets confused sometimes," Bill said. "You know, thinking people who died years ago are still around, mixing up nurses with family members."

"Does she have some kind of persecution complex? Like she thinks the Mafia or someone is out to get her?"

He shook his head. "Not that I know of. You're the first one who's said anything about her being afraid of someone. I've chatted with her a lot, and she's never said anything like that to me."

But maybe she hadn't trusted Bill. Maybe she'd felt she could only trust her daughter and closest friends with her suspicions. The only problem was . . . none of them were alive.

"What's wrong?" Bill asked.

"She wrote me a letter," I blurted out. "In it, she said that other patients have been killed by some guy, but she was the one he wanted. She thinks she's next."

Bill just stood there, no expression on his handsome face.

I went on. "So, what do you think? Are the people who have died recently just the ones you'd expect not to make it?"

He stared down at me, suddenly serious. "Geriatrics has lost six patients in the past two months. That's almost double the normal number. I'd been thinking it was kind of strange—so many, so quickly. But that doesn't necessarily mean—"

"Don't doctors study the body, do an autopsy or something to see if the person died of natural causes?" I asked.

"Only if the family requests it or the attending physician suspects foul play. These were all old people who were pretty sick. If they hadn't died the day they did, they'd have probably died a few months or a year later." His voice was gentle, and he came over and sat beside me on the bed. "Babies are born, other people die. It's part of life, Maggie."

"I know," I said shakily. "I guess I just don't like the dying part, especially if it's violent."

"Like in your dreams?" he asked softly.

My head snapped up, and I stared at him for several seconds before I could speak. "How did you know about my dreams?"

"Word gets around," he said, touching my arm gently. "A couple of the nurses on night shift saw Dr. Berman chase after you last night."

"So now the whole ward knows?" I asked, my face hot with embarrassment.

"I doubt if the other patients are aware. It's just that the nursing staff pass along important information during daily staff briefings. The new shift has to know what to expect from their patients—if someone's blood pressure is up, or someone's had a lot of pain during the night . . . that sort of thing. I sat in on the morning meeting."

I took a deep breath and fought back tears of humiliation.

"Maggie? Is something wrong?" he asked.

"No . . . I guess I'm just tired," I lied. I hadn't wanted him to know about the terrors. "I want to rest."

He nodded. "I've got to get going anyway. I have fourth-floor duty tonight."

He leaned a little closer, but I turned my face away. I didn't feel like being kissed.

After a moment he stood up and walked toward the door. "I wouldn't worry too much about Mrs. K. She's going home tomorrow anyway. She'll feel more secure in her own house."

"Sure," I said, but I couldn't let go of the chilling words of her letter.

I didn't feel like being around anyone in the hospital that night. But I did feel like talking to a special friend. I found out how to place a long-distance call from my room and folded up a five-dollar bill inside my wallet to save it for the phone bill when it came. I figured the research project probably wouldn't pay for my personal telephone calls.

I dialed Elly's number and waited while the phone rang. By eight rings I felt more miserable than before and was about to hang up. Then Elly answered.

"Yeah, what?" She sounded out of breath.

"It's me, Maggie," I burst out. "What have you been doing?"

"Running, what else? Hey, it's great to hear from you! Are you settled into your new apartment?"

"Not really," I groaned.

I'd wanted so badly to talk to her . . . and now the story of the accident, of my parents leaving me in Chicago with Dr. Berman, of our plans for getting rid of my terrors came tumbling out. The words sounded hopeful, but like always Elly saw right through them.

"That's terrible! The dreams are getting worse, aren't they? You don't normally have them during the day, do you?"

"No, but—"

"You could have been killed!" she muttered darkly. "I hope this doctor can do something for you. How are your folks taking all this?"

"Okay, I guess." I twirled the phone cord around my finger and lay back on the bed. "They left yesterday. My mom said she'd call in a couple of days to check on how I was doing and see if I'd changed my mind about staying. She really freaked out when I said I wanted to stay here."

"All moms get hyper when their kids are sick," Elly said.

"Yeah, but Chicago . . . there's something about this city that makes her crazy." I shook my head. "Remember when we were supposed to take that field trip to the Art Institute last year? She wouldn't sign the permission slip, said it was too dangerous."

"So, she worries about you."

"I know. But you have to admit it does seem a little obsessive."

"All mothers are obsessive."

I laughed. "Who are you? Dr. Spock?"

"No," she teased, doing one of her best impressions, "Dr. Ruth. How's your love life, dearie?"

I told her about Bill, how I hoped he was interested in

85

me the same way I was about him. After talking a little while longer, I said that I had to go to sleep. I didn't want to make Dr. Berman stay up the whole night again.

Since the terrors always seemed to come two or three hours after I'd fallen asleep, I could plan on getting them over with early. Then she could go home to her own bed for the rest of the night.

"Give me your room number, and I'll call you in a couple of days," Elly promised.

We said good night, and I felt better, having heard her voice. I punched in Dr. Berman's extension, but a stranger's voice answered.

"Dr. Berman isn't available right now. This is her answering service."

"This is Maggie Johnson. She told me to call when I was ready to go to sleep."

"I'll contact her, Miss Johnson," the woman said.

With a sigh, I hung up. I brushed my teeth, undressed, and put on my Grateful Dead night shirt—a birthday gift from Elly. By the time I'd stretched out on the bed and pulled the covers up to my chin, Dr. Berman was knocking on my door.

She stepped into my room and smiled tiredly. "I see you're all ready. Have you decided the terrors aren't so bad after all?"

"After the day I've had," I grumbled, "they might even be fun."

I must have slipped into my shallow, stay-alert dozing mode. Around eleven o'clock, I woke myself up without thinking about what I was doing. Dr. Berman's head was nodding, and her eyes were closed. I had to go to the bathroom, so I plucked off the sensors and slid out of bed.

The woman was immediately awake. "Are you all right, Maggie?"

"I'm fine. I don't think I'm going to dream tonight. Maybe you should go home."

"Are you positive?"

"No," I admitted, "But I'm pretty sure. Go home, I'll be okay."

She was waiting for me when I came out of the bathroom after using the toilet and washing my face with cold water.

"I'll hook you back up and let the floor nurse know she should check on you every half hour or so."

I nodded.

"I'll stop by and see you in the morning," she promised.

nine

I was right: I didn't sleep or dream. I stuffed two pillows behind my head, fell back on them, and stared morosely at the ceiling. Exactly twelve acoustical squares crossed the ceiling going one way and ten ran in the other direction. Each one was dotted with tiny holes. I tried counting them but gave up at three thousand eighty-nine because I discovered I'd been counting some of them twice.

With a bored sigh, I took out Mrs. K's letter and reread it. In the dim light of my bedside lamp, it looked even more like the demented ravings of a lonely old woman. I stuck it back beneath my pillow, closed my eyes, and drifted . . . but didn't sleep.

After a while I thought about what Dr. Berman had said about my being real little and something awful happening that might have started the night terrors. I remembered when I'd been seven and woke up in my mother's arms in an ambulance. Blood was all over her, and she was crying.

"Don't cry, Mommy," I said, trying to comfort her. "You'll be all right."

Then I realized that *I* was the one on the stretcher and more blood was on me than on her. A man in a pale blue uniform was pressing gauze to my face to stop the bleeding. I had no idea what had happened. I just remembered being chased by the crazy woman and trying to get away from her.

It turned out I'd escaped from her all right—through a window, which happened to have been closed at the time. It wasn't the last time it would happen.

Then a flash of something else came to me. I was in the principal's office in the first school I went to. He and my mother were arguing, and I sat on a tiny, plastic chair in the corner, pretending to play with letter blocks while listening to the grown-ups and wondering why they were so angry.

"I'm very sorry, Mrs. Johnson," the man snapped. "No one can register a child without a birth certificate."

"It was lost in our last move!" she wailed.

"Send to the town clerk's office in the community where she was born," he said. "They'll mail you a copy."

"But that might take *weeks!* I want her to start with the other children."

"We can't bend the rules, Mrs. Johnson."

I remembered thinking that I must have done something wrong, that maybe it was *my* fault the paper they were fighting about was missing. I was glad my mother didn't tell the principal that. I wouldn't have wanted him to think I was bad or stupid.

Then I was drifting further back . . . back to a time before I went to school. One night, I woke up feeling afraid and confused. I staggered into the living room, looking for my parents, and found them sitting close together on the couch, whispering. Although they were probably just trying not to wake me, I was curious and wanted to find out what they talked about late at night when I was in bed. Before either of them could see me, I hid behind the couch.

"It was a dumb thing to do," my father rasped out, pounding his fist on the wooden arm. "I told you that from the beginning, Francine. You'll be running for the rest of your life!"

"Time will change things," my mother said, tears running down her cheeks. "They'll give up."

"Would *you?*" he demanded angrily. "Would you quit if it was—"

Suddenly, he'd stopped talking, and there was an awful silence. I crouched down low, hugging my knees, praying he wouldn't see me. But he appeared suddenly around the corner of the couch and yanked me to my feet. I'd never seen him that mad before.

"What did you hear?" he demanded, shaking me so hard my teeth rattled. "What did you hear, Maggie . . . Maggie . . . Maggie . . . ?"

I couldn't remember anything more. The vision drifted away like a paper sailboat on a breeze-blown lake. I tried to sink further back into my life. Back to when I wasn't much more than a baby . . . but I couldn't. It was as if I'd run up against a cement wall. I could see nothing on the other side.

Suddenly I became aware of a soft sound in the room with me. Stiffening, I listened with my eyes still shut. It came again—the gentle shushing of fabric rubbing against itself, like the legs of new blue jeans. I tried to breathe evenly, but my pulse sped up, and I had to force myself to inhale. I sensed someone nearby . . . someone moving around my bed . . . moving closer to me.

Was I asleep? Was it the crazy woman of my dreams?

No, I thought. *She'd be screaming and flashing her knife in my face even before I opened my eyes. Sneaky isn't her style.*

Slowly I opened my eyes. A shadow moved across the dark hospital room. Maybe it was one of the nurses, come to check on me. As I watched, the dim shape slowly pulled open the top drawer of my bureau and started searching through it.

I watched, still afraid but getting angrier by the second. It shouldn't matter that I was in a hospital. No one had a right to go through my personal things. While the figure's back was turned, I silently lifted the blankets away and sat up.

90

"Nurse?" I asked tightly. "What's wrong?"

The figure froze. It was too dark to make out its face, or even tell if it was a man or woman. But I sensed that whoever it was, it wasn't a nurse. The person wore dark clothes, not hospital whites or modern pastels. It was as if he or she had dressed not to be seen.

"Who are you? What do you want?" I demanded loudly. As I spoke, I reached for the nurse's call button beside my pillow, but it wasn't where I'd left it.

The figure didn't answer, and an icy finger of fear crept up the back of my neck. Sweat trickled down my spine beneath my night shirt.

"You have no right going through my things!" I hissed. "Get out of here!"

Without warning, the shadow ducked and seemed to dissolve into the thick darkness. I watched the closed door, guessing whoever it was would try to escape now that I'd spotted him. But the door didn't open. I heard fumbling sounds from my bedside table.

Quickly, I pushed myself up from the bed, and the sensors snapped off of my skin. I didn't know what I was going to do for sure, but I wasn't going to stay in the room with an intruder. Planning to get out first, then block the doorway while I screamed for help, I dove for the door.

My fingertips barely brushed the cool metal of the doorknob before something heavy and hard crashed down on my head. I can't say that I saw stars like in the cartoons, but there was a brilliant, almost pretty explosion of light before everything went dark.

"What happened?" a voice demanded. "Did you fall?"

Someone was dragging me up off of the floor. I reached out and caught hold of the edge of the steel bed frame. My head buzzed like the dismissal signal at my old school in Winona, and my knees kept buckling. I couldn't seem to get them to hold me up.

"Yes," I mumbled thickly, "I fell when . . ." My brain started to clear. "No . . . no!" I blurted out. "Someone came up behind me . . . hit me with something."

The nurse who was helping me to my bed let out an impatient snort. "I'll get Dr. Berman. You rest in bed."

"Aren't you going to call the police?" I asked. "Someone just attacked me!"

I touched the sore spot under my hair at the back of my head. My fingers came away wet, red blood slicking over my fingertips.

"Wait!" I called to the nurse. But she'd already left.

I looked around for the call button that I hadn't been able to find in the dark. With the light on, I could see the wires hanging raggedly from the wall. The button had been yanked off.

A sour taste of bile welled up in my mouth.

Pushing up off of the bed, I staggered toward the door and into the hallway while I clutched the back of my head.

The nurse ran back to meet me. "What are you doing out of bed?" she demanded, seizing me by the arm.

"I'm not delirious. I'm not imagining things," I gasped. "Look, look at my head!" I bent down, flopping my hair forward.

"Oh, darling, how'd you ever do that to yourself?"

I wrenched my arm away from her. "I didn't do it to myself, you jerk!" I shouted, losing my temper. "Someone *attacked* me!"

She gave me a pitying smirk. "Betty!" she shouted down the hallway at the other nurse. "Call Dr. Berman . . . at her home if you can't get her any other way. And get the on-call physician up here to take care of Miss Johnson's head."

"What do I tell Dr. Berman?" the other woman asked.

"Tell her that Miss Johnson had another nightmare, and she hurt herself."

"No!" I screamed. "I didn't do anything to myself. How many times do I have to tell you? Someone was in my room, and whoever it was slugged me on the head!"

"Now, calm down, dear," she cooed. She gripped my arm harder this time and wrestled me down the hallway.

"Now, be a good girl and hold still until we get you patched up. You'll just bleed more, wiggling around like this."

"But the person in my room—"

"Dear, I've been here all night. Don't you think I'd have seen someone if they tried to get into your room?"

"Sure, if the creep walked down the middle of the hall past the nurse's station while whistling 'Yankee Doodle Dandy'! But what if he sneaked up the back stairs?"

She sniffed. "That's ridiculous—people sneaking around in the middle of the night smacking patients over the head?"

I groaned out loud. There was no use arguing with her. I'd have to talk to Dr. Berman and hope she understood.

I was shaking and couldn't stop now. Maybe Mrs. K's paranoia had gotten to me—all her talk about people getting murdered in the hospital. Then I touched my bleeding head, and I knew I wasn't crazy.

I tried to call Elly as soon as the doctor who'd patched up my head left, but got no answer. I slammed my phone down and sobbed into my fists. I knew that Elly would have believed me, no matter how strange my story.

Dr. Berman arrived a few minutes later. When I told her about the intruder in my room, she was more encouraging than the nurse, but not much.

"It's hard to believe that you could fall in a way that would hit this part of your head," she said, lightly touching the bandage the other doctor had applied.

"That's because I *didn't* fall," I repeated for the thousandth time through gritted teeth. "Someone broke into my room and clobbered me! I keep telling everyone that!"

She sat me back down on the bed and came around in front of me, wearing a solemn expression. "Do you remember any part of a dream?"

"I wasn't dreaming," I insisted. "I never got that deep into sleep."

She hesitated, taking a long breath. "Sometimes when we first wake up, we confuse our leftover dreams and waking thoughts with reality. It's very easy to do, Maggie. We're somewhere between our subconscious and conscious lives."

"No," I insisted. "I wasn't dreaming or confused or anything like that. Someone was in my room, and they panicked when I tried to block their escape."

Dr. Berman sighed.

Then I remembered about my trip back through time.

"I didn't dream last night," I repeated. "But I did remember some more stuff from when I was little."

"Yes?" she asked, taking her notebook from her briefcase.

"The first time was back when I was seven years old, when I crashed through the bedroom window during a night terror. I woke up feeling confused and thinking, at first, that my mother was hurt. But the blood was mine. She'd probably been holding me while we waited for the ambulance."

Dr. Berman was writing frantically. "Anything else?"

"Yes, I went further back, to when my mother registered me for kindergarten."

"You'd have been about five years old then."

"Yes," I said, straining to force my memory to work. "My birth certificate was missing, and the principal wouldn't let her leave me at school until she'd registered me correctly. I felt guilty because I thought maybe it was my fault. I was always losing things when I was little—my toys, a mitten, a scarf. They just seemed to disappear, and my parents always had a fit."

"Did your mother blame you for losing the birth certificate?"

"She didn't say she did, but I thought I might have. I liked to draw with crayons, and sometimes when there wasn't any drawing paper in the house, I sneaked old mail out of the wastebasket or grabbed anything I could get my hands on."

She nodded. "This is good, Maggie. Do you understand now that you can't blame yourself for the missing certificate? All children enjoy coloring and are apt to do it in places they shouldn't. It's normal . . . the sort of thing that little kids do."

"I guess," I said. But I was sure there was something more, something terribly important that I wasn't focusing on. "One time, my folks got real mad at me for spying on them. They were arguing, and my father accused my mother of running away from something."

Dr. Berman nibbled her pencil eraser. "Did she leave home as a young girl? Did she run away with your father to get married? Or might she have been pregnant and afraid to tell her parents?"

I shook my head. "She would have been almost thirty by the time she had me. My parents got married in their late twenties."

"Well . . ." She smiled and shrugged. "Eventually this will all make sense. In the meantime, just try to relax and keep an open mind. If you remember anything from earlier in your life, we may find a key to all of this, and to your terrors."

"What about the person in my room? The person who attacked me?"

She pursed her lips and studied me. "The nurses told me they saw no one, either going into your room or leaving."

"So you don't believe me either?"

She observed me solemnly. "Was anything missing? Money? Your purse or any jewelry? Anything of value?"

"No."

"You see," she said in a kindly voice, "there's no reason why anyone would want to hurt you, Maggie. It doesn't make sense."

I felt sick to my stomach. The truth was, someone *had* hurt me. There was no reason to think he or she wouldn't come after me again!

"You're up early this morning," came a voice from the doorway.

I jerked around to see Bill step into the room, wearing a solemn expression. It was barely six in the morning, and he looked like he'd had a bad night, too.

Dr. Berman patted me on the shoulder. "Why don't you take it easy today. Spend some time with the other patients in the lounge. Maybe get Bill here to walk you down to the cafeteria for a big stack of pancakes." She looked pointedly at him, and I wondered if she was ordering him to keep an eye on me.

Anger bubbled up in my veins. I bit down on my lower lip and spun away from him. I didn't want him to see how furious I was with her for not believing me and for setting me up this way.

I waited until she'd left the room, then sat down hard on the edge of the bed and stared into space.

In spite of my resolution not to cry, tears trickled down my face. Why wouldn't anyone listen to me? Why?

A minute later, Bill stepped over beside me.

"Looks like you've already heard the news."

"What news?"

Holding my chin in one hand, he turned my head to look me in the eyes. His long face was grim and troubled. Then his eyes widened as they settled on the crown of my head.

"Hey, why the bandage?"

I told him about the intruder.

"Wow," he breathed, "that's terrible."

"What news?" I repeated, a sense of dread growing in my gut.

"We can't talk in the hospital," he said quickly. "What happened to you last night changes things. Do you think you could walk a half mile or so if we take it real slow?"

"My collarbone is broken, not my legs," I reminded him dryly.

"Then get dressed," he said. "I'll meet you at the bottom of the east stairwell."

"All right," I agreed.

I waited until he'd left, then grabbed my jeans, a sweatshirt, underwear, and sneakers, and ran into the bathroom. As I dressed, I wondered what they did to kids who went AWOL from a hospital.

ten

I'd never cut classes at school. And as petty crimes go, this felt ten times worse. I met Bill at the bottom of the Personnel Only stairs, grateful that Nurse Hitler hadn't grabbed me on the way down.

He looked even paler than before, and his eyes seemed glassy and distant.

"What's wrong?" I asked, falling into step as he started walking north on a busy street marked STATE STREET.

Without answering me, he took a quick left. I had to jog to keep up with his long legs, and my chest tightened with tension . . . or maybe it was just the tape around my ribs pulling.

"Come on, talk!" I shouted.

"I came to see how you were taking the news about—" He broke off and swallowed. "Anyway, I realized you hadn't heard, so I thought we'd better talk somewhere outside the hospital."

"Get to the point," I said impatiently.

He put his head down and strode across the street, anger and sorrow building in his blue eyes. "Mrs. Krane died last night."

I stopped breathing. "She *died?*" I gasped.

He nodded.

"But she was getting better! She had pneumonia, but she was supposed to go home because she was going to be okay! Geringer said so."

He winced. "I know. I worked on her floor for two

98

days last week. I can usually tell when we're going to lose a patient. There's something about them, a change in the way they act, as if they know . . . it's hard to explain."

"She didn't seem like that to you?"

"No," he said firmly. "I mean, she was old, and I guess she didn't have a lot of years to live. Maybe only two, but maybe ten . . . who knows? I just don't think it was her time," he finished softly.

I felt as if I were going to get sick, but I kept on walking. I couldn't tell how far we'd come or where we were headed. There were a lot of tall buildings. Traffic streamed by noisily, and the air smelled of automobile exhaust, people's bodies, and a slightly sour aroma that I connected with urine and dirty pavement—which made my stomach feel even worse.

The street sign said LA SALLE. We crossed over a bridge that spanned a river.

"You mean, she was *murdered?*" I whispered, at last.

He nodded, then shook his head as if he couldn't make up his mind. "I'm not sure."

"How did it happen?"

"I don't know the details. All I could find out was she supposedly died in her sleep. A nurse found her while making her routine rounds at 3:00 A.M."

"I can't believe it," I choked out, tears creeping up into my eyes. "Remember the letter I told you about? When I took it from her, she was sleeping but she looked fine."

Bill jerked to a stop, grasped my hand, and stared at me. "You said she was sure a man was going to kill her and she claimed other people had been killed by him?"

"Right. But she also said that she was the one he was really after, and she didn't know why he'd kill anyone but her."

"That doesn't make sense," he mumbled.

"No," I admitted. "It doesn't. Especially because she

99

said that she trusted him. So he has to be someone she knew."

"She knew him, and knew he was going to kill her. . . , " Bill repeated. He closed his eyes for a second, then reopened them and straightened his long body to gaze off across the street. "Maybe he knew all the victims. Maybe there's some kind of connection that will give him away."

A bus roared past, leaving us in a cloud of choking, black exhaust. "Maggie, I don't know how much we can depend on what Mrs. Krane said in her letter, but something terrible is happening at North Central. I'm sure of it now."

I looked around automatically to see if anyone was listening. This must have been why he'd wanted to get away from the hospital before we talked.

"But who would want to kill a bunch of old people?" I whispered hoarsely.

"We don't know that it's *only* old people," he pointed out. "I've noticed that deaths in Geriatrics are higher than normal. I'd have to check records for each department from a year ago and compare them with those for the last few months to see if there was a marked difference."

I leaned closer to him. "Can you do that? I mean, are you able to get hold of patients' files and stuff?"

"Not very easily," he admitted, staring at me solemnly. He squeezed my fingertips hard, and I could feel his hand shaking. "There's something else worrying me, Maggie."

"What's that?" I liked the way we were sharing secrets, even if they were morbid ones. We *knew* something no one else knew, and that made me feel closer to him. "What else is worrying you?" I repeated.

"It seems strange that on the very same night Mrs. K died, someone broke into your room and cracked you on the head."

I nodded slowly, feeling as if my veins had suddenly been pumped full of liquid lead. If he'd wanted to start walking again, I don't think I could have moved. People brushed past along the sidewalk, giving us strange looks for blocking their way.

"Bill—" I began weakly.

"Yeah?"

"You think the person in my room was looking for that letter, don't you? You think it was the killer."

He took a deep breath. "I don't know. Have you mentioned the letter to anyone but me?"

I shook my head. "Maybe he saw Mrs. K writing it," I suggested.

"Yeah, and maybe he had to wait until she was asleep to get it away from her—"

"But he saw me take it before he had a chance to," I finished for him in a shaky voice. "I don't know . . . I still don't understand why anyone would murder people in a hospital."

He shook his head. "You see horror movies about that sort of thing. You know, using people's brains or hearts for some kind of freaky scientific experiment . . ."

"I mean in real life."

"Well, there have been cases of mercy killings."

I swallowed. This was something I'd read about before, but I'd never given the newspaper stories much thought. "You mean, old people were killed to keep them from suffering?" I whispered.

He nodded. "In one case a nurse shut down life-support systems for several of her patients because she believed they were suffering too much."

"But Mrs. Krane wasn't in pain," I pointed out. "She might have gotten confused sometimes, but I think she wanted to go on living. If she hadn't, she wouldn't have asked her friends and family for help."

"I know. And most of the other patients weren't hurting bad either. So it has to be something else."

I was starting to feel a little weak from hunger. "Let's get something to eat," I suggested. "Maybe we can think better on a full stomach."

Bill looked around quickly. "Gee, I didn't realize we'd come this far. We're almost to Clark Street. Come on, there's a McDonald's a few blocks from here."

We walked past a few more blocks of tall buildings. Now that we were moving slower I could look around a little more. I'd never been to Chicago, or any really big city, but somehow the size of the buildings, crowded sidewalks, and blaring car horns didn't intimidate me. In fact, I felt almost at home. Maybe I'd been a big-city girl in an earlier existence, I thought, grinning at how silly that sounded.

When we entered McDonald's it was totally different from any of the others I'd seen. A '60s Corvette was parked in the middle of the dining room, and the place was jammed with rock 'n' roll memorabilia—Elvis, Little Richard, and Frankie Avalon dolls; life-sized figures of The Beatles; minijukeboxes at every booth.

We sat down with our food, and Bill punched a button. Bob Seger belted out "Old Time Rock & Roll."

"This is the coolest place," I gasped.

Then I remembered the shadowy figure in my room and felt the weight of something the size of a chair crushing down on my skull.

"I know," Bill mumbled through a mouthful of egg-and-sausage sandwich. "I come here a lot. Listen, I don't want to spoil your fun, but I think I'd better take a look at that letter."

"Sure."

He took another bite. "Where is the letter now?"

"Under my pillow."

He wiped his mouth hurriedly. "Come on, finish eating. We'd better get back to your room fast and move the note to a safer spot."

I stuffed the rest of my Egg McMuffin into my mouth and trashed our papers. We ran all the way back to the hospital. My ribs didn't hurt as much today as they had the last time I'd tried to run, but I still had to support the arm on the side of my broken collarbone with my other hand.

"We can't get back in the way we came out," Bill said. "The stairway door's always locked from the inside for security. We have to go through the main entrance."

He flashed his student volunteer card.

"I'm a patient," I told the guard.

He inspected my badge and made me write my name and my doctor's name in a log.

Without speaking we took the elevator to the third floor and rushed down the hallway. I stuck my hand under my pillow and fished around for the smooth, paper rectangle. Pulling my hand out empty, I looked at Bill.

"It's got to be here somewhere," I said. "I know I left it under the pillow, and the sheets haven't been changed, so it couldn't have gotten tossed in with the laundry."

He flipped over the pillow, then tugged the top sheet off. The bed lay bare . . . no letter.

I stared at him. "Someone came in here after we left and took it."

"Looks like it."

"What are we going to do?" I asked frantically. "Now the killer knows that *I* know Mrs. Krane thought she was going to be murdered."

"Maybe there's another explanation," Bill muttered tightly. But his eyes were dark with worry.

"Well, who else would have taken the letter?" I insisted. "What do we do?"

"There's nothing we can do," he said grimly. "We have no proof of any of this. Besides, everyone around here figures Mrs. K was sort of loony. Even if we still had the letter, it wouldn't carry much weight with the administrator or the police."

"I suppose so," I said.

"We'll just have to come up with something more solid before we can go to anyone."

After Bill left for school, I searched my whole room, just in case I'd moved the letter without thinking about it. But at the end of an hour, I was convinced that it was gone.

103

I felt hollow inside, as if my heart had been stolen with the letter. I'd only spoken with Mrs. K once and seen her twice—the second time while she was sleeping. But she'd been a sweet old lady, and I felt furious that she'd trusted me . . . and I'd done nothing to help her. Someone had snuffed out her life as easily as I blew out candles on a birthday cake. Worst of all, they'd gotten away with it.

It didn't matter whether she had only a few years or months or even days left. The way I figured about my own life—every hour, every minute counted. I'd have been spitting mad if someone robbed me of even ten minutes.

I walked down to the lounge. Jerry, a boy from Detroit who'd come for surgery after a football injury, was watching cartoons. Dean and Marie were cuddled up in each other's arms on the couch, whispering and giggling. I wondered if they'd try to see each other after they left the hospital. Or maybe their hospital relationship was like a summer romance and would end sweetly but finally on the last day of their stay.

I plucked a book off the shelf and tried to read, but the words refused to focus. Evil things were going on in this place. I could feel their hungry presence in my bones. Wicked, mysterious, deadly things—and I was caught in the middle of them.

It wasn't just Mrs. Krane and her nutty ravings that had somehow had come true. There was something more. I felt as if this *place* itself had a special power over me—a power to dredge up my past.

Before I'd come to North Central, I'd never been able to remember anything about being a little kid. But now, every couple of hours, something new flashed through my brain like a clip from an old movie. I saw myself as a little girl sitting in a kindergarten classroom, munching on graham crackers and sipping milk through a thin paper straw from a little red-and-white carton. Somehow I knew I'd liked the color blue, and

I wore frilly dresses even when my friends wore blue jeans.

Then there were flashes of the hospital—an office, a hallway, a waiting room. I could no longer tell my age, or even if I were part of the visions, but they seemed disturbingly vivid. *If the hospital itself isn't pulling memories out of me, then I must be bonkers,* I thought.

I was more scared than I'd ever been. I couldn't wait for Dr. Berman to come by at four o'clock, as she'd promised.

Lunchtime came and went. Two patients from Adolescent Surgery were released and headed for home, wheeled down the hallway with balloons ribboned gaily to their wheelchairs and their parents lugging flowers, teddy bears, and assorted gifts down the hall.

After they were gone, all of us left behind were quiet. It was like losing friends who'd helped you through bad times. Worse than moving, because we knew we'd never see them again.

I went back to my room and stretched out on my bed. Almost immediately, another flash hit me: a huge white house with a big porch. To one side of the front door, a summery green swinging bench hung by chains.

I shook my head violently and sat up. I didn't dare take a nap. My brain was so active I might slip into a terror, and I didn't want to be sidetracked now. I had to find out more about Mrs. Krane and her murderer.

I pushed up off the bed, walked down the hall, and took the stairs up to Geriatrics. Peeking through the wired-glass pane in the door, I waited for an orderly to pass by. Then I streaked across the hall and into the old woman's room.

Luckily, a new patient hadn't moved in yet. But the room had been cleaned, all of Mrs. K's personal items were gone, and the beds had been freshly made up. It was almost as if she had never existed. Tears welled up in my eyes. It didn't seem fair.

105

Sinking down onto the floor, I sobbed softly. I touched the side of her bed and shook my head as the room blurred.

"I'm sorry I didn't listen to you," I croaked out. "I'm sorry, I might have saved you."

She'd trusted me! And I'd let her down in the worst possible way. It didn't matter that we'd known each other only a short time. It didn't matter that she thought I was Lucy. I was all she had . . . all except for a nephew, I remembered, who'd come to see her only once during her three-month stay.

I blinked away the tears, knowing I couldn't just stay in this room, mourning her on the floor. Bracing myself with the hand on my good side, I started to stand up. But something shiny, stuck between one leg of the bed and the wall, caught my attention.

It was thin and bright, almost colorless, and hard to see. Crawling under the bed, I pulled it out.

A syringe.

I turned it over in my fingers, careful not to touch the needle point. It had been used. A thin residue of liquid clung inside the tube.

I studied it, frowning. Nurses and medical technicians were so careful these days about disposing of needles. With the fear of AIDS and all, it seemed strange that one had been carelessly dropped on the floor and no one had searched for it. I wondered if it even made sense that Mrs. K would be getting injections for pneumonia, which she'd already recovered from.

"So, it's *you* again!" a voice bellowed from behind me.

I jumped straight up, my heart rocketing into my throat. Without thinking about what I was doing, I shoved the hypo into the hand-warmer pocket in the front of my sweatshirt.

"I just came to say a final good-bye," I said, turning to face Dr. Geringer.

He stepped toward me, his face on fire with anger. His

106

eyes looked like a prowling tiger's, amber and intent on its victim.

"Listen, you!" he shouted. "I don't know why you're even in this hospital, since you're well enough to go tripping through the hallways at all hours!"

He grabbed the back of my shirt and dragged me into the corridor. A nurse coming from the opposite direction hastily ducked into a room as he marched me toward the elevator.

I thought he was going to put me on it. *Okay by me!* I thought. I couldn't wait to get away from him.

He surprised me by stepping inside the elevator and pulling me along with him. Punching the button marked Adolescent Surgery, he stood stiffly as the doors closed in front of us.

I looked around, glad to see other people were already on board. A man and woman carrying flowers and a stuffed giraffe stared at me as if I were a convict under armed guard. I turned my head, avoiding their eyes.

They stepped off on the fourth floor. When the doors slid closed again, I jerked around to face Geringer, knocking his hand loose.

"I didn't do anything wrong!" I shouted at him. "Mrs. Krane was a nice old lady, and she wasn't ready to die! I just want to find out what happened to her!"

He glowered at me. "What are you talking about?"

I was so angry I was no longer thinking straight. I said the worst possible thing. "I'm talking about murder! Mrs. K told me that someone wanted to kill her and someone did! Someone who's killed other patients at North Central! I don't know who or why yet, but I'm going to find out, and when I do I'm going to make sure plenty of people—like the families, know what happened!"

His eyes widened dangerously, and his hand shot out toward me. I lunged out of range, only to realize that he'd been reaching for a red button on the control panel. As soon as he hit it, the elevator jerked to an abrupt stop.

107

"Do you have any idea what you're saying?" he snarled.

I swallowed, suddenly aware of a horrid possibility. The note had said *he*. If the *he* had been a doctor, it might logically have been Mrs. K's doctor—Geringer.

I looked around the closed compartment. I obviously wasn't in the best situation to accuse someone of being a serial murderer. If anything happened to me, Geringer could invent whatever story he liked and the police would probably believe him. After all, he was a respected surgeon, and I was just a hysterical teenager who had wacky dreams.

I chose my words carefully. "I said, someone has been killing patients. . . ."

Geringer stared at me for so long I thought he'd never move again. Then he lifted a hand to his brow and rubbed his thumb hard into the deep creases, like someone who has a really bad headache.

"Do you have any evidence other than the gossip of an old woman to prove your claims?" he asked in a whisper-soft voice.

"Listen, *you* keep chasing me off Geriatrics and away from Mrs. K's room. How am I supposed to get hold of evidence?"

"You belong in your own ward," he said gruffly.

"I told you, I have permission to leave Adolescent Surgery. Anyway, I was visiting her during regular visiting hours. She didn't have anyone else."

"I know she didn't," he said softly. "Unless you count that nephew of hers."

I looked at him. The depth of his caring for his patients showed in his eyes. Suddenly his voice sounded tired and troubled, and he didn't look capable of hurting anyone. I almost felt like patting him on the back and saying, "It's okay, you've had a rough day."

"So you have nothing," he repeated.

There was the note, but it was gone. I didn't want to

mention the syringe until I'd had a chance to discuss it with Bill. I nodded. "Nothing."

He looked at the elevator control panel, then at me, then at his big, soft surgeon's hands. "I think we need to talk somewhere else. Why don't you come with me to my office for a few minutes?"

"How about the cafeteria?" I suggested. "I'm awful thirsty."

"Fine."

He started up the elevator again. When we reached the first floor, he led the way. "Do you want a soda?" he asked.

"Root beer," I said automatically, then chose a table while he went through the line.

He came back with a cup of hot tea for himself and a large styrofoam cup of frothy soda for me. His eyes looked distant, as if he were thinking of something else . . . a place or time or person far away.

I needed to get him back on track fast. "You wanted to know if I have anything to prove there's a killer loose in this hospital," I reminded him.

"Yes," he said.

"Mrs. K not only told me that someone was trying to kill her, she wrote me a note."

"She did?" His eyes narrowed. "Can I see this letter?"

I took a sip of soda. "I don't have it any more. Someone took it from my room."

He scowled. "That's interesting."

I nodded and looked up from my cup to find him studying my badge. "My name's Maggie Johnson," I said before he could call me Margaret.

He smiled. "Maggie. That's a nice name. A little old-fashioned, but nice."

I decided to ask the question that had been bugging me ever since I first ran into Geringer. "Why have you been so hot to chase me out of Geriatrics?"

He looked thoughtful. "Because I'd questioned a

109

couple of my patients' deaths before you came along. Although it's impossible to predict with absolute certainty if an elderly or very sick patient will live for long, usually a doctor has a sense about these things." He shook his head. "I was suspicious of any unauthorized person on the floor."

"Then *you* figure someone has been killing people, too?"

"I don't . . . don't know what to think," he said in a low whisper. He dunked his tea bag one last time, then pulled it out of the steaming water by its string and rested it on his saucer. "I just haven't been totally convinced that these people died of natural causes . . . and Mrs. Krane seems the most questionable of all," he said darkly.

"Then why haven't you done anything?" I demanded loudly.

A couple of people turned to look at me.

"Sorry," I said, lowering my voice. "I'm just upset."

"I understand, so am I." He hesitated. "If it makes you feel any better, Maggie, I asked the families if they'd agree to autopsies. But they all refused."

"I guess people in mourning don't like the idea of their loved ones being dissected," I said.

"True," he sighed. "But it seems odd, all the same, that not one of them gave permission for an autopsy. It sure might have answered some questions. Anyway, I also went to the hospital administrator and told her my suspicions."

"And?"

"She said that I was imagining things."

I laughed out loud. "That's what people tell me all the time!"

He smiled. "The point is, if I had some real proof to show Mrs. Anderson, she might take the matter more seriously." He stared at me hopefully. "Tell me about this note. I have a feeling that even if you still had it, no one would take it seriously since Mrs. Krane was

110

quite senile. But it might give us some clue to follow up on."

"Mrs. K wrote that some man was trying to kill her and that he'd do it before she was released, which was going to be the next day."

"Did she say anything that would tell you who this person was?"

"No, just that it was a man, and she'd trusted him."

"Someone she knew." He pondered this for a moment. "Well, it's something. You're sure you didn't just misplace the note?"

I turned around so he could see the bandage.

"My God, the thief did that to you?" he gasped.

"I guess it was the same person. Whoever it was snuck into my room while I was sleeping to look for the note. When I caught him, the creep bashed me over the head and took off." I winced, remembering the pain. "He didn't get the note then, but came back for it the next morning while I was out of my room."

"You told the floor nurse about this?" he asked.

"I told everyone who'd listen, but they think I dreamed it and just fell."

He shook his head. "This person sounds desperate to cover his tracks. Maybe that's good. Maybe he'll stop killing now."

"And what about Mrs. Krane and the people he's already killed? Are we supposed to forget about them?" I asked tightly.

"No ... at least, I can't ..." He looked away for a long moment. "But do you have any idea how terrible this could be for their families? It's traumatic enough to lose a grandmother, uncle, or father to natural causes after a long illness. But we'd have to tell these people that their relatives were murdered while under the care of our staff."

"Could be a little embarrassing for the hospital?" I commented. "If they all decide to sue, it could cost the hospital a lot of money."

"The hospital be damned!" Geringer shot back, anger flushing his cheeks again. "It's the *people* I care about!"

I watched him with interest. He really did seem to care.

"I'm going to look into this," he continued in a firm voice. "I'm going to get to the bottom of this, Maggie. Will you trust me enough to promise me one thing?"

"I don't know," I answered cautiously.

"Bring me anything you might stumble on. I don't want you to put yourself in further danger by trying to hide evidence."

I chewed my bottom lip, thinking about the syringe in my pocket. There was still a nagging doubt in my mind. I wanted to trust Geringer all the way, but did I dare?

I decided to keep the syringe to myself, just a little while.

eleven

I wanted to give Bill the syringe before I was tempted to hand it over to Geringer.

He'd asked me to trust him, and the strange thing was . . . I did. Sort of.

I mean, I was still real suspicious of my feelings toward him. They weren't logical. You don't just trust people because they tell you you should. They have to earn it. Bill had, Geringer hadn't. So I had to find Bill, which might not be easy in a hospital the size of North Central. He could be anywhere.

I figured he'd be in school until after two o'clock. So I spent the early afternoon hanging out in the lounge with the other patients. I took a quick walk around Bill's favorite departments between three and four, but couldn't find him. I stopped by the volunteer services office and left a note asking him to come see me on his break. Then I went back to my room to rest and hope that he'd get my message.

Lying on my bed, I tried to think back to my kindergarten days, then further, deeper into the years. But I kept hitting the gray wall. Nothing existed before that day in the principal's office. It was as if Maggie Johnson had sprouted out of nowhere at five years old.

I gave up and returned to the lounge. Dinner trays had been delivered. The nurses first served patients who wanted to eat together, then took the remaining meals to those who were staying in their rooms.

I sat with Gloria, Tandora, and Sammie—three auto accident victims. Tandora's boyfriend had been killed in the accident that had broken both of her legs. She told us that she was driving that night because she was less drunk than he was.

Tandora kept crying and saying, "We should never have gotten in the car. . . . We should never have gotten in . . ."

There was nothing we could say, because she was right.

I tried to change the subject. "So when are you guys going home?"

"Next week," Gloria said. "I can't wait to see Chuck, he—"

Sammie shot her a *shut up* look. Talking about boyfriends, under the circumstances, wasn't cool.

Luckily, Valerie showed up right then and passed out menus for the next day. We had to check off our choices. I marked pancakes, applesauce, and milk—for old times' sake. For lunch I decided on fish sticks and baked beans. For dinner . . . chicken breast, mashed potatoes, and a salad. Totally uninspiring food—but hey, my heart really wasn't in eating.

It was getting late when Bill walked in.

"I have to talk to you," I said as soon as he came over to the table where I'd been putting polish on Tandora's fingernails.

We walked to the far end of the lounge near the bookshelves and away from the TV where most of the kids huddled watching a rerun of *Roseanne*.

"What's up?" he asked.

"Doctor Geringer caught me in Mrs. K's room again."

"What were you doing there?"

"I suppose I just went to say good-bye. But I found something." I slipped the hypo out from my sweatshirt and dropped it into the pocket of his lab coat.

He looked down at it, frowning. "A needle?"

"Someone dropped it under her bed. I thought, you

114

know, if a person used it on her in a hurry and . . ."

"You think she might have been injected with something lethal?" he gasped.

"It's possible, isn't it?"

Bill scowled down at his pocket. "Yeah, I guess. But you'd think a killer would be more careful and not leave behind evidence."

"I know. That bothered me, too. But maybe someone interrupted him, and he couldn't go back without arousing suspicion. He might figure the cleaning crew would dispose of it without thinking anything was strange. Can you find out what was in it?"

He tipped his head to one side. "I have a friend in the lab. He'll run a chemical analysis for me."

"Good."

"But what will we do if it *is* something toxic?"

"I'm not sure," I said slowly. "Maybe we should go to Mrs. Anderson."

"How do you know the administrator?"

"I don't. But Geringer mentioned her name." I told him about the strange chat I'd had with Geringer in the cafeteria.

"He's tough to figure," Bill said. "I wonder if he's telling the truth about having gone to her."

"I believe him."

"Why?"

I shrugged. "I don't know. There's this way he . . ."

I caught a two-second vision of something . . . something from a night terror, I thought. But my brain must have been short-circuiting, because there was no way Dr. Geringer could have any connection with my dreams. He'd never appeared in one, it was always the screaming crazy woman.

"What's wrong?" Bill asked. "You looked for a second as if you'd seen something awful."

"Nothing," I said quickly. "I must be tired. I didn't sleep much last night."

He looked at the round-faced clock on the wall. "It's

only eight o'clock. But if you want to sleep . . ."

"I think I can, but I have to call Dr. Berman to come sit with me."

"I can stay with you until she gets here," he offered.

I smiled at him. He was so nice. "Okay."

I told the duty nurse that I needed her to call Dr. Berman for me. Bill walked me the rest of the way down the hall. I was so exhausted it didn't hit me until I was in front of my room that we'd been holding hands since we'd left the patients' lounge.

He squeezed my hand, as if to say, *You're going to be all right. Hang tough.* I smiled at him gratefully through my exhaustion. If he kisses me, I thought, I probably won't even feel it.

He pushed open the door to my room and stepped aside to let me through first.

One look at the room, and I was suddenly wide awake. "No!" I wailed.

The place looked as if the entire varsity football team from Winona High had scrimmaged in it. My books lay scattered on the floor. My makeup and the pretty bath powder Elly had given me as a going-away present had been knocked off the dresser onto the carpet. Bill's balloon bouquet lay deflated on the bed. My stuffed bear was jammed head-first into the trash can. His fluffy white innards were strewn all over the room.

Bill let out a wry laugh. "I thought girls kept their rooms neater than guys!"

"I didn't do this!" I snapped at him.

"Somehow, I didn't expect you had. Oh man, what a mess." He turned toward the bed and asked, "What's that?"

A piece of construction paper lay on my pillow.

"I don't know," I murmured, picking it up.

I unfolded the bright red paper, the kind we used to cut into valentine hearts when I was in grade school. Inside, someone had pasted rows of capital letters cut from a newspaper. The letters spelled out:

116

Bill snatched it out of my fingers. "This doesn't make any sense."

"Oh, yes it does . . . it means whoever's killing people in this hospital wants me to take a hike."

"I don't mean that. I mean, by leaving something like this in your room, the person is drawing attention to himself. It's like saying, 'Well, maybe you weren't sure that someone was knocking off patients before, but now I'm telling you that I'm for real!' "

"You're right," I said. "Clobbering me over the head was a smarter way to scare me off, because everyone thought I was making it up."

"Maybe the person who left the warning is betting that Dr. Berman will think you wrote this note, too."

I shook my head. "No. She might suspect that I'd imagine something but honestly believe it to be true. She won't believe that I've gone to all the trouble of pasting letters on construction paper and trying to intentionally trick her."

"What are you going to do?" Bill asked.

"Let's just pick up and keep quiet about this until you find out what was in that syringe."

"Are you sure?" he asked, looking worried.

"No, but it's the only thing I can think of for now. I sure don't want to take this to Geringer until we know something more about that needle. And I'm not sure why, but I'd like to find out more about Geringer, too."

Bill sighed. "Okay, but be careful."

I grinned at him, feeling silly and playful in spite of the danger . . . or maybe because of it. "Why?"

He looked surprised. "Why?"

"Yeah, why should you care what happens to me? Because I'm one of *your* hospital's patients?"

He put his arms around me and smiled. "Naw, you're more special than that."

"Special?"

He laughed. "I don't go around kissing every patient in this place, you know."

I played along, draping my arms around his slim neck. I could smell a spicy after-shave that I hadn't noticed him wearing on other days. "Kissing? Like that little peck the other day?"

"No," he murmured thickly, lowering his head and shoulders to bring his lips in touching range of mine. "Like this."

For a long blissful minute, I floated in Bill's arms. Slowly I became aware of someone clearing her throat, for what sounded like not the first time.

"I thought the message was you were tired and wanted to sleep?"

I shoved Bill away and jumped backward. "Dr. Berman! I thought you were in your office, or at home, or . . ." I was blushing, and I knew it.

"Or at least not here?" She smiled good-naturedly. "I was down on the first floor."

Bill stepped farther away from me and coughed embarrassedly. "I . . . we were just . . ." He waved his arm to indicate the condition of the room.

Dr. Berman drew in a sharp breath, as if she'd been too interested in what she'd caught us doing to notice the surroundings. "What happened here?"

"When we came back from the lounge, this was what we found," I told her.

"This is outrageous!" She tapped her pen angrily against her notepad. "No one heard anything?"

"We haven't gotten a chance to ask," I admitted.

"Well, I'll certainly do some asking!" she huffed, rushing out of the room.

"I hope she doesn't do a Geringer job on those poor nurses," I mumbled.

While she was away, Bill helped me start picking up. Strangely, in all the mess, nothing much had been broken. Only the balloons and my bear.

"Man, someone sure went wild in here," he mumbled after a while.

Wild.

The word reminded me of my night terrors. The wild woman—that was how I always thought of her. What would I do if she ever became real? If she stepped out of my terrors and came after me? Had she paid me a visit in the flesh?

I shook off the feeling of her knife blade piercing my flesh. There was still something important missing . . . some clue that would make sense of everything. My dreams, patients dying when they weren't supposed to, someone attacking me and stealing a letter to a dead daughter from an old lady . . . a carefully trashed room.

A few minutes later Dr. Berman stomped back into the room, in an obviously rotten mood.

"I can't believe that no one heard a thing!" she fumed. "And the two nurses who should have been able to see anyone coming onto the floor claim they saw no unauthorized visitors in the last five hours." She shook her head in disgust. "Someone isn't telling all. Someone knows something," she muttered.

I felt guilty for hiding the needle and the note from her. But she hadn't believed me when I'd told her about my head, and I didn't think I could stand watching her shrug off my theories about Mrs. Krane's killer. It was better to wait, I reasoned, wait until Bill and I had a bundle of proof.

I fell asleep pretty quickly, undoubtedly because I'd slept so little the night before. I felt safer now that Dr. Berman was watching over me. Still, I didn't lapse into the night terror right away. As always it took a couple of hours of fitful dozing to come to me. In the meantime, my mind drifted between conscious and subconscious half-sleep.

I was back in kindergarten again, painting on a big easel with huge wooden-handled brushes, splashing gallons of dripping primary-color paints across thin newsprint. I was

119

painting a tree, a sun, and grass with flowers poking up through it. I was painting these things because the little girl at the easel beside me was painting them. I thought, *If I draw what she's drawing, I won't get in trouble.*

What I really wanted to do was create a scene all in black, with a little girl at the end of a tunnel. She'd be alone at first. Then I'd paint in the other person—a woman with glowing eyes and deadly claws at the end of flailing arms.

"Stop! Stop!" I'd paint in the word balloon over the woman's mouth.

I looked at the wild woman through my dream eyes. Something about her made me feel sorry for her, which was ridiculous because she was the evil one, the one chasing and threatening me.

Then I sensed that I was shrinking, or perhaps growing still younger. I was in a tiny room with only one window, which was covered by a heavy, dark shade—the plastic kind that pulls down to keep out light when you want to sleep in the morning.

I was playing with an empty Quaker oatmeal box and wooden spoon, drumming on the box and singing loudly, "When the saints come marching in!"

Someone came into the room and said, "Maggie, sweetie, time for your dinner."

I looked up, and it was a woman with straight, shoulder-length brown hair and a plain face. At first I didn't recognize her as my mother. It must have been before she'd cut her hair and started dying it. She picked me up under my arms and hauled me to her hip, cooing at me as if I were a little baby. But I knew I wasn't a baby, not really. I might only have been three or four years old, but I wasn't a baby.

"Go back further," I told myself.

But this time the wall was strong and solid. No matter how hard I tried, I knew that I wouldn't get beyond it tonight. I let go of the past and drifted up through the cottony layers of years to the present.

When I at last woke up, my stomach was knotted and I was sweating. I wondered if I should try to get past the wall again. What if, on the other side, I found unpleasant answers to my questions?

The next morning I woke up to find Valerie napping in the chair where Dr. Berman had been the night before.

"You sure look younger than when I went to sleep," I teased her.

I didn't say she looked uglier, which was what I'd really been thinking. Dr. Berman must have been in her thirties, but she had the sweetest, prettiest face. Valerie was big-boned and had a terrible complexion, but she must have been kind-hearted to spend so much time at the hospital without pay. That's what counted.

"A good night's rest does wonders for a girl." She yawned and stretched. "Are you done sleeping?"

"Yeah," I said. "What happened to Dr. B?"

"She was called away on an emergency. She asked me to sit in for her until you woke up." She stood up and stretched again, then looked around with a puzzled frown.

"Your room looks different."

"I rearranged some stuff," I told her quickly.

I wondered for a moment if there was some way Valerie could help me. After all, she knew the hospital better than anyone, and she got around to every floor with her book cart every day.

"Do you remember that old lady in Geriatrics, Mrs. Krane?" I asked.

"Sure." She sighed. "I felt awful when I heard about her."

"Me too," I murmured, my throat threatening to close up with sadness at the thought of her. "Did you see her yesterday? The day she died?"

Valerie scrunched up her face in concentration. "I didn't get to her end of the floor. I had to take inventory that day."

"So you didn't see her at all?"

"No."

I shook my head, disappointed because I'd hoped Valerie might have spotted someone suspicious in or around her room.

"Did you see her nephew yesterday?"

"No." She hesitated. "Not yesterday. But today I ran into him on the elevator. He was heading up to her floor. I'll bet he came to pick up her personal things."

I thought about the words in Mrs. Krane's letter. She'd distinctly mentioned her fear that a *man* was going to kill her. Someone she knew—a family member, a friend, a hospital employee?

"Did he look upset?"

"Oh, I don't know," she murmured. "I'd say he was pretty much in a world of his own, like he was shutting out everything around him. Maybe he was in shock. He didn't believe she was gone. Lots of people react to death that way."

"The nurse told me Mrs. Krane had no one else in the world. No other family."

"I never saw anyone else in her room," Valerie admitted. She studied my expression. "What's the matter? Why are you so interested in her?"

I wanted to confide in her. She might be a big help. But I no longer trusted anyone except Bill, and maybe Dr. Geringer. Maybe. "I just thought she was sweet, that's all," I murmured.

Valerie nodded. "Well, you know what they always say at funerals. . . ."

"What's that?"

"At least she didn't suffer. At least she's with Jesus now."

I smiled at her dimly. "I'm glad she didn't suffer, too."

"Hey, how's it going?" Bill called from outside in the hallway.

"Fan-tas-tic," I ground out between my teeth.

Sitting cross-legged on the bed, I drew a needle and dark brown thread through the plush fabric in my hands. The thread snagged for the tenth time in two minutes, and I groaned in frustration.

"I *hate* sewing!" I screamed.

"Why are you doing it, then?" He was laughing at me.

"I want my teddy bear back!"

He came over to sit on the bed beside me. Leaning close, he kissed me on the lips casually, as if it had been our way of saying hello every day for years. I grinned up at him to let him know I liked it.

"So, you find out anything?" I asked in a hushed voice.

"About the syringe?"

"Yeah." He was silent for a moment. I glanced up again to study his expression. "You found something!"

"Sh-sh-sh," he warned, glancing toward the door as he pulled out the syringe, now wrapped in a plastic baggie. "I don't think we should spread this around, not yet anyway."

"So?"

"It was insulin. Patients with diabetes have to take it intravenously."

I was disappointed. "You mean it was just an ordinary medicine?" I held out my hand to take the syringe from him.

"No," he whispered so low I could hardly hear him. "Mrs. Krane wasn't diabetic. And even if she was, the syringe was large enough to hold an overdose, according to my friend in the lab."

I swallowed, then swallowed again, staring at him. "You mean, the insulin would have killed *anyone* who was injected?"

"If the syringe had been full at the time it was used on her, the stuff would have been lethal." Bill looked at me, a mixture of fear and excitement in his eyes. "This is it, Maggie. We've got proof!"

My mind was racing. "Almost. We can't say for sure that the syringe was full. But the overdose would show up in an autopsy, wouldn't it?"

"Sure. A pathologist studies the body to see if there are any signs of violence or hidden causes of death."

I remembered what Geringer had said about trying to get a family member to agree to an autopsy. "We can tell this to Dr. Geringer. Then he can ask the nephew for permission to do the . . . oh, no." I'd forgotten something very important. "But he's a suspect. If he killed her, he'll never agree to one. . . ."

"Just what I was thinking," he murmured.

We were both quiet for a long while. All this talk about murder had sent a chill through every bone in my body. I felt the need to touch something living. Something breathing and real.

I reached out and slipped my arm between Bill's elbow and his side, then rested my head on his biceps. . . . I couldn't reach his shoulder. He silently supported me, moving his thumb soothingly over the soft skin on the back of my hand.

Suddenly I felt very sad. In a few days, whether or not we found out what had happened to Mrs. Krane, whether or not Dr. Berman and I had gotten to the bottom of my night terrors, my parents would lose their patience and insist that I join them in Dayton.

But it wouldn't be home for me. Home was . . .

"Geez," I groaned, squeezing my eyes shut.

"What?"

"I don't know where my home is anymore," I moaned.

"Huh?"

"I left Winona, so that's not home. And by now my parents have found a new apartment. I don't even know where it is. I don't know what it looks like."

"You'll get used to it," he said gently.

I always had before—but this time felt somehow different. I shook my head. "You don't understand. It's so weird—what I was thinking just now."

He frowned at me. I guess I must have sounded pretty strange.

"See, *this* feels like home to me," I said.

"Chicago?"

"No . . . the hospital. I feel as if I know all the parts of North Central the way you know your bedroom is the second door past the bathroom in your house. I can smell and feel everything about it. Even when you and I left to have hamburgers, it was still here for me." I touched my forehead.

Bill looked even more confused. "I'm not sure what you mean."

"I feel . . ." It was hard to put into words, because it sounded insane. "I feel as if I've been here before," I let the words out in a single breath.

"But you haven't. You said you'd never even been in Chicago!"

"I know!" I let go of him and pressed my fingertips against my closed eyelids. "It's just that this feeling is so strong. Sometimes when I walk around a new floor I've never been to, I can predict which way the corridor will turn, or how many offices are off of it."

"That's creepy," Bill breathed.

"I know." I took a few deep breaths, trying to calm my racing heart.

"Do you believe in one person living different lives?" Bill asked tightly.

I looked up at him over my hands. "What do you mean? Like reincarnation?"

"I guess . . . I don't know. Just the idea that a person might have been around before, then she died and came back again, maybe as the same sort of person, or as someone completely different . . ."

"That's reincarnation, any way you cut it." I thought for a moment. "I suppose it's possible."

We looked at each other in disbelief.

"It could be just a coincidence," he said at last. "May-

125

be you were in a similar building once. Maybe it was designed by the same architect and it . . ."

He let the thought go. It didn't make much sense to me, either.

"So what are we going to do about the insulin?" I asked, pocketing the syringe. "I say we go to the administrator now."

He shook his head and blew a puff of air between his lips. "Mrs. Anderson's in San Francisco for a week at a health conference. Until she gets back, why don't we find out a little more about Geringer. If someone's been pumping killer doses of insulin into patients, it might not have been Mrs. K's nephew. Why would he murder all those other people?"

"Even Mrs. K didn't understand that," I added. "She said so in her letter."

"Maybe it was Geringer or some other doctor, working on his own. Maybe the guy took it upon himself to play god with patients he thinks medical science can't help anymore."

The ultimate ego, I thought. Doctors got swelled heads sometimes, but deciding for a patient to end his or her life was sick. Somehow I didn't think Geringer could kill, but something inside of me was still curious about him.

"He said I could come to him any time I wanted, and we could talk," I murmured.

"Good," Bill said. "This time, see if you can get into his office."

"Why? You think he's going to leave vials around marked 'Insulin—Lethal Dose'?"

"No, but if he's the killer there might be something we could use. I'll wait in your room. Call me there right before you go in to see him. Make some excuse about needing to telephone your folks. I'll find a way to get Geringer out of the office for a few minutes so you can look around."

For some reason, the idea of tricking Dr. Geringer and nosing around his personal things gave me a creepy

126

feeling. But if he were trying to cover up killing patients, then he must have been the one who slugged me over the head and trashed my room. It was the least I could do to repay him.

"All right," I said. "Let's go."

"Wait." Bill put a hand out to stop me. "What are we going to do with the syringe?"

I remembered what Geringer himself had said about keeping possible evidence in a safe place. "I'll hide it where no one will find it."

"Not in your room."

"No," I agreed, "not in my room. Somewhere too hard to guess. Maybe in the new construction, but in a part where they aren't working very much yet."

"Good idea. Up on one of the top floors," Bill suggested.

I left him in my room and took the elevator to the eighth floor, got out, and ran down the hall to the place where the construction crew had broken through the old wall. A thick plastic sheet covered the opening. I ignored the No Admittance sign, pushed the curtain aside, and stepped through. No one seemed to be around.

Avoiding heavy steel cables and blocks of cement, I moved past an elevator cage. Not much farther along, I came to a small, walled room with a lot of open pipes sticking up through the floor—probably a future bathroom. I stuffed the plastic bag down one of the pipes, then stood up, checking to be sure no one walking past could see the syringe.

Perfect, I thought.

twelve

"I don't have much time," Dr. Geringer said, scowling at his watch as if he blamed it for his tight schedule. "I have to complete my rounds, then see patients at my office."

"But you said I could come talk to you. . . ." I stared down at my hands as if I was deeply disappointed in him.

"Of course you can, but I . . . my . . ." He shifted feet. I could feel him studying my sorrowful expression. "All right, if it's that important. But let's make this fast, Maggie."

His office was in the professional building across the street from the hospital. The two buildings were connected by an enclosed footbridge, so you didn't have to go outside in bad weather or fight city traffic to get from one side of the street to the other. While Geringer stopped at his receptionist's desk to ask her for messages, I helped myself to her phone. I dialed the hospital number, then quickly hit my room extension number.

"I'll be a little late for lunch," I said into the receiver. It was our code—to let Bill know that I was about to enter Geringer's office. Not waiting for him to respond, I hung up.

Geringer was watching me when I turned around. "What was that all about?" he asked.

"The nurses on my floor get bent out of shape if I don't keep them posted."

"I see," he mumbled, still staring at me as if he guessed

something was up but couldn't put his finger on what it was. "Well, come on in."

We walked into a tiny room crammed with books, files in manila folders, and a blizzard of loose paper. His office didn't look at all like I'd expected. I'd figured him for a neataholic; everything would be as stiff and orderly as he was. But this place looked almost as bad as my room after it had been ransacked.

"Sit," he said abruptly.

I plopped down in the nearest chair and let my eyes roam the shelves of thick, leather books. I'd bet anything that they contained dozens of ways to kill someone without being found out, but that didn't mean Geringer had killed anyone.

"What's on your mind, Maggie?"

My glance drifted to a photograph on his desk. It was a baby picture of a child about a year old, in pink rompers with white bows in her hair. Beside it was another photo—Geringer with his family.

He was standing beside a young woman, and between them posed a toddler, grinning at the camera. The two little girls could have been the same kid. They looked a lot alike. In the second photo the girl was somewhere between two and three years old.

Behind the Geringers was a huge white Victorian house. It had a homey, wraparound veranda with pretty carved railings and a porch swing. Baskets of brilliant red geraniums hung behind their heads.

I couldn't take my eyes off of Geringer's face in the picture. As he smiled into the camera, he looked so young and handsome. His right arm encircled his wife's slim waist, and his other hand rested on the child's curly head.

A disturbing warmth rushed through my veins, then was just as quickly gone. Although I couldn't identify its source, it left me shaking inside.

I looked up at Geringer. He seemed eons older than he'd looked in the photo.

"What is it?" Geringer asked sharply.

I jumped. "I . . . I was just looking at your photographs. They're very nice," I added quickly.

He reached over and abruptly flipped each one face down on his desk. "Why did you want to talk?" he growled.

I ran my tongue over my lips. "I wanted to ask you something about Mrs. Krane."

"What?"

"Her nephew . . . do you know him?"

"Just to tell him about his aunt's condition. I spoke to him once at the hospital, soon after she was admitted, and again over the phone the morning she died."

"Was he very concerned for her? I mean, do you think he really cared what happened to her?"

Geringer's frown deepened. "I don't know why this has anything to do with what we discussed before," he rumbled. "Are you implying that—"

There was a sudden commotion in the outer office. Geringer turned his head to listen.

I could hear Bill's voice along with those of a couple of kids from the adolescent ward. They were chanting something about patients' rights.

The desk intercom clicked on, and the nurse's voice blared, "Doctor, you'd better come out here!"

"Excuse me," Geringer said, already out of his chair and racing toward the door.

I counted ten seconds after he'd swung the door closed behind him, then dived for his desk and started sifting through the papers on top of it. There were a lot of notes on patients. Under those were some files, then advertisements and samples from pharmaceutical companies, a memo to the staff from the Office of the Administrator announcing her absence to attend the conference in California, a technical journal and correspondence with the American Medical Association—but nothing mentioning Mrs. Krane or insulin.

Frantically I pulled open drawers and began working my way through them, moving aside pencil stubs and scribbled notes that meant nothing to me. In the back of my mind I knew that if Geringer was the killer and he caught me going through his personal stuff, I'd be next on his list.

Vaguely aware that the noise from the outer office was growing softer, I searched faster. The center drawer over the kneehole had nothing; the top right drawer, nothing either. The middle right drawer was nearly empty. There was only one three-inch thick file.

I pulled it out and looked at the label on it. It read, STEPHANIE.

This must be a patient he's had for a real long time, I thought. None of the others were over an inch thick. And he must have developed a personal interest in her to think of her by just her first name.

But as I flipped through the scraps of paper inside, I could see there were no medical records beyond a birth certificate—the kind hospitals issue for souvenirs to new moms with their baby's tiny foot and handprints.

There were also bills and receipts, and long lists of names with phone numbers. Some were in Michigan, but others were in Ohio, Indiana, Missouri, and other states. . . . The most distant was in California. And near the bottom was a photocopy of a pencil sketch of a little girl. I wondered if it was the same child as in the photo.

Reaching across the desk, I turned over the larger of the two gold frames. Three people stared back at me: Dr. Geringer, Geringer's wife, and the little girl. When I held the sketch beside her, there was no doubt that she was the same child as in the sketch.

Her name is Stephanie, I thought.

I hadn't looked closely at Mrs. Geringer before, but I did now. Her eyes were her best feature. They were a pale, iridescent lavender, and they sparkled with happiness. She rested her sun-flushed cheek against her husband's shoulder. Her left hand gently clasped the toddler's fingers as she gazed contentedly into the camera lens.

131

For some reason, though, her expression seemed all wrong. The features looked oddly familiar, but her happiness was out of place.

Why should I think that? I wondered. She was a young mother with a healthy child and a handsome young doctor for a husband.

An unexpected flash of terror sliced through my nerves, and I dropped the photograph with a weak cry. The frame hit the corner of the desk and clattered to the floor.

"No!" I gasped. "No!" I groaned louder.

It wasn't possible! But I knew, with a chilling certainty, who that woman was. Mrs. Geringer was the wild woman of my night terrors! But how did she get into Dr. G's life . . . into his reality at the same time she lived in my imagination?

A muffled scuffing sound came from just outside the office door. Shakily, I shoved the file back inside the drawer even as the door swung open.

"Maggie?" a voice issued out of the black void closing in around me. "Maggie, are you all right?"

I choked back the sour bile that had risen into my throat, and realized I was still sitting in Geringer's chair. "I'm . . . I feel dizzy. I'd better go."

I blindly lurched toward the door, but Geringer caught me by the arm and forced me into a leather chair.

"You look as if you're ready to pass out, young lady. Sit down. I'll get you a drink of water."

He didn't have to leave the room. There were paper cups and a carafe of ice water on a side table.

"Here, drink this," he said, lifting the cup to my trembling lips.

I sipped the cold liquid, beginning to feel better, my head clearing, my vision blurring less. I saw the photo lying face down on the floor.

"I knocked off your photograph. It was an accident. I'm sorry," I mumbled.

With an almost tender gesture he replaced the frame on his desk and set the other one upright as well. "Do

132

you know anything about a teen patient demonstration that had been planned for today?" he asked. "Something about adding pizza to the hospital's menu and ending curfews?"

So that was the interruption Bill had arranged. I shook my head. "Is Stephanie your little girl?"

Geringer nodded slowly, his eyes latching onto mine, drilling through them and into my soul. "How did you know my daughter's name?" he asked.

"One of the nurses mentioned it," I lied quickly.

The muscles in his face relaxed a little. "Yes, that's Steph in both those photos."

"That's an old picture," I said, choosing my words carefully. "You don't have any recent ones of her? She must be almost high school age by now."

A streak of pain crossed his face. "She would have been. She's no longer . . . she's gone."

He still loved her so much, he couldn't bear to say the word *dead*. I looked at the family photo again. Apparently he and his wife had never had another child.

I still hadn't stopped trembling, and I couldn't take my eyes off of the woman. How could that pretty lady be the same screaming witch who'd chased me through my night terrors?

Then another thought occurred to me: How would a mother react to the death of her only child? Would she wail out her helpless grief? I could imagine her face ravaged by agony. It looked just like the wild woman's face in my dreams!

But where had I seen Mrs. Geringer before? And how had I known about her tragedy years before I set foot in Chicago?

My head hurt worse than ever. I dropped my face into my sweating palms. I had to get out of here. This was too much; I must be cracking up.

"You came here to ask me something," Geringer said as I started up out of my chair. "What is it?"

I sat down again. "I . . . I wanted to know when Mrs.

133

Krane's funeral is scheduled. I'd like to go if I can find a way."

He looked at me, puzzled. "You really did like her a lot, didn't you, Maggie?"

"Yes," I whispered. "I want to say good-bye to her."

"I'm afraid that's impossible," he said in a sad voice.

"Why?"

"Her body was cremated this morning."

It took a long moment to sink in. Until that second, Mrs. K hadn't felt totally gone. But she was ashes now—there wasn't anything more gone than that. And what was worse, there was now no way of proving she'd been injected with something that had killed her. There was nothing left to analyze.

"Isn't that kind of fast?" I choked out.

"Yes, it is." He scowled at his desktop, and I wondered if he was already thinking of a way to get rid of me so he could finish his rounds. "It's very unusual, but that's what the family wanted. Maybe it's easier that way, not having to mourn for so long."

"By family, you mean the nephew."

He looked at me with a puzzled expression. "Yes. Is something wrong?"

I decided to test him. "I think the nephew killed her."

"What?"

"I think he murdered his aunt."

He laughed. "You're kidding, right? You think her only living relative did it?"

"But," I interrupted, "you said—"

"I told you that I was suspicious of a few patients' deaths. But there was absolutely no motive for Matthew Krane to kill his aunt. She had no money of her own. They weren't even particularly close, so they'd probably had very little opportunity to pick fights over the years."

"There must be *some* reason she died," I reasoned, watching his face for a reaction.

"Yes," he said calmly, "there must be."

134

"But you don't think it was natural causes . . . do you?" I demanded.

"I'm not able to say anything just yet. I have to look into all of this further," he said bluntly.

I stood up. "I'm feeling better now. I'd better leave."

He gave me a strange, sad look, then glanced away. "Come back if you want to talk more, Maggie."

"Why?" I blurted out. "You never seem too thrilled to see me."

He shook his head and shrugged. "I don't know. Maybe it's because of Stephanie. She'd have been about your age if she hadn't—" He still couldn't get it out. "I'd like to think she'd have turned out as smart and pretty as you."

I was shocked. His face had softened with his words, and I suddenly felt so terribly sorry for him I wanted to fling my arms around his neck and tell him that I understood why he had to be so cold and gruff . . . why he couldn't let his emotions through. But why should anything I say matter? I thought. It was his Stephanie he missed, and she'd died a long time ago.

Bill was waiting for me in the hallway around the corner from Geringer's office. I was maxing out on body trembles by the time I reached him.

He grabbed me and pulled me through a doorway into a small waiting area filled with orange plastic chairs and two-year-old magazines.

"What did you find?" he asked tightly.

"I don't know."

"What do you mean, you don't know?"

"I mean what I said!" I snapped at him. "I found some stuff, but it wasn't what I was looking for."

He put an arm around my shoulders, pulled me down into a chair, and sat beside me. "Calm down. It's all right. Just tell me what you saw."

After a few minutes of deliberate slow breathing, my heart stopped racing. I drew my tongue over my lips and began. "Geringer acts really disturbed sometimes."

"What do you mean, disturbed?" Bill asked. "Like upset, or like mentally unbalanced."

"Maybe both," I said. "It seems he lost a child a long time ago. He keeps a file with documents and correspondence about her in a special drawer. Her picture, standing with him and his wife, is on his desk."

"I don't think there's anything strange about that. Lots of people keep photos of their loved ones even after they've died," Bill commented. "And the file could be old family letters that mention her. Sort of a memorial."

"No," I said firmly. "Some of the notes were dated ten years or more ago. Others were only four or five years old. I saw one that was written just last year, but I didn't have time to read any of them before Geringer came back."

Bill scowled at the floor. "This doesn't make sense. Why would relatives or friends still be writing about her if she'd died that long ago?"

"I'll tell you something that makes even less sense," I whispered. "The woman in the photo . . . Geringer's wife . . . she's the woman in my nightmare."

"The one chasing you?"

"I'm almost positive." But it seemed incredible to me, too. I couldn't keep my hands still. Clenching them in my lap, I worked them into tighter knots as I spoke. "She has the same eyes, the same shape face. She even looks the same age."

"But you've never been in Chicago! You've never met Geringer before you came here."

"More important, I've never, *ever* met his wife." I felt as if I were slipping faster into the abyss of my madness. But there *had* to be an explanation!

"What about the patients who died? Did you find out anything about them?" Bill asked at last.

"Nothing."

He nodded. "So we still have only the syringe."

I sighed. "Maybe that's enough to at least get an investigation started."

"Right," Bill said. "As soon as Mrs. Anderson gets back, we'll give her the syringe and tell her everything that's happened."

I sighed. "Well, we may not know anything more about Mrs. Krane's death, but we know something more about my night terrors. They're getting weirder all the time, considering the fact Mrs. Geringer is in them."

"Maybe they are, and maybe they aren't," he murmured thoughtfully.

"What do you mean?" I asked.

"If we assume that there's no such thing as reincarnation . . . I mean, if we're strictly scientific about this, then you must have known Mrs. Geringer or someone who looks like her at some time in *this* life."

"Okay," I agreed slowly.

"So, if you can trace *her* past, maybe you can find the key to yours."

"But I *know* my past," I objected. "And she's not in it. Unless maybe her daughter died in some awful way and it made the Chicago newspapers. Maybe I saw her photo, and she was crying, hysterical or something."

Bill nodded. "Yeah. And her face scared you and somehow stuck in your mind."

"But I still don't know what's giving me night terrors!"

"Dr. Berman says something traumatic set you off years ago. How far back can you remember now?" Bill asked.

"Maybe to three or four years old . . . before I was old enough to go to school."

"And what do you see before then?"

"A wall . . . just a black wall." Tears of frustration trickled down my cheeks.

Bill grasped my arms and gave me a gentle shake. "You have to remember, Maggie."

"But if it's so terrible that I've blocked out the truth all these years, maybe I'm better off *not* remembering!" I sobbed.

He pulled me close to him and held on, letting me cry against his chest.

"I guess you have to decide what you want," he whispered. "If you don't go all the way back, you'll never be rid of the terrors. If you do, you may learn things you'd rather not."

I closed my eyes and gripped him hard. "I know," I murmured. "I know."

Dr. Berman came to my room at eight o'clock. "The nurse told me you'd had a rough day," she said gently. "She thought you might want to go to sleep early, or talk a little before you went to bed."

I smiled at her. She was so nice. I was sure that she had no idea what I was going through or that people were being murdered right under her nose.

I shrugged but didn't say anything while she attached the electrodes to my face and head, then fooled with dials on the polygraph. At last she switched off the overhead light, leaving the room bathed in the dim red glow of the sleep lamp near my bed.

"There's something I need to know," I said after a long silence. Just the thought of what I was about to say sent a chill through my bones.

"Shoot," she said, cheerfully.

"About Dr. Geringer . . ."

"Has he been harassing you again?" she asked, a touch of irritation in her voice.

"No . . . actually, he's being almost friendly . . . for him." I looked at her. "What happened to his little girl?"

"I don't think that's any of your—"

"It *is* my business," I insisted, sitting up in bed. "I was in his office today. There's a picture of him and his family. His wife is the woman in my dream!"

"Mrs. Geringer?"

"Please, please tell me," I begged her.

Dr. Berman frowned at me. "The woman in your dream

must be someone who just looks a lot like Mrs. Geringer. You can't really believe that it's *her* chasing you."

"I'm sure of it. The wild woman's even the same age as the woman in the photo."

Dr. Berman glanced away from me for a long moment. She cleared her throat and fixed me with a hard look. "Maggie, you're not jerking me around, are you? You're not making all of this up because you think I'll be more interested in you and you'll be able to stay longer at North Central if you act mysterious and . . ."

"No!" I cried. "You have to believe me! You have to tell me about Geringer's family! What happened to Stephanie?"

"All right," she said slowly. "I only know the rumors I've heard around the hospital since I first came here. And that was six years ago."

She was silent for a moment, her face wrinkling in concentration. "Geringer supposedly completed his internship in this hospital," she began. "This is where he met Rebecca Fields. She was a nurse in the labor and delivery area, helping to bring new babies into the world."

I found it difficult to think of stony-faced Dr. Geringer as a young intern, and in love. But having seen the old photograph helped. I could imagine a young nurse falling for the tall young man with dark hair and intelligent eyes.

Dr. Berman was talking without hesitation now. "They dated for just a year before marrying. And the following year, Rebecca left nursing to stay home and care for their baby daughter, Stephanie.

"People said they were the perfect couple. Rebecca kept her strong ties with the hospital, promising to return to nursing as soon as Stephanie entered school."

A strange sensation swept over me as I listened. It was as if I'd heard the story before, although I knew that was impossible—because I was sure I'd remember the end.

"Mrs. Geringer often brought her little girl to the hospital and walked her around to visit old friends in the different departments. They frequently showed up to have a quick lunch with Dr. Geringer."

"Sounds like they were a very close and loving family," I murmured.

"You never know . . . maybe things weren't as smooth as they seemed. I'm just telling you what I've heard. . . ." She took a deep breath.

"At any rate," she continued, "the family's future seemed to be guaranteed rosy, until one day when Rebecca brought her daughter with her to visit. This time, as she often did while chatting with the nurses, she let Stephanie play in the waiting room with toys that were kept there to amuse young patients. The receptionist could see her through a glass panel, and the child was probably so accustomed to the routine she wouldn't have wandered off anyway."

"How old was she?" I asked tensely, sensing that the story was about to take a tragic direction. Part of me wanted to delay Dr. Berman's words, while another urged her on.

"Three. Stephanie was three years old."

A sliver of fear pierced my heart. But I couldn't quite focus on its cause. "What happened then?" I asked, clutching her arm.

She looked with concern at me. "Are you all right? You're trembling, Maggie."

"Go on! Go on!" I begged her.

"I will, but calm down. This was a long time ago and really has nothing to do with you."

I nodded to reassure her, but I didn't believe it. I didn't believe that my nightmare woman and the woman in the picture were two different people. And if they *were* the same, then I knew Rebecca from sometime in my past, and I had to find out the connection. I had to find out what she'd done to me that was so horrid I'd shut that moment out of my life!

Dr. Berman went on cautiously, as if she were afraid of upsetting me even more. "What happened next seems to be . . . well, pretty confusing. But the short form of it was, a young woman entered the waiting room and grabbed the child."

"She kidnapped her?" I cried.

"Yes, and she apparently got away with her even though the receptionist saw what happened and screamed for the child's mother. Rebecca Geringer took off after the woman, and the receptionist alerted security. Somehow the woman eluded everyone and escaped with Stephanie."

I had to try three times to swallow over the rock-hard lump in my throat. "Oh, God, her baby . . . the woman stole her little girl. . . ."

"Yes," Berman said solemnly.

"Did they ever find her?" I didn't want to think about what happened to the kid, but I couldn't help it. I'd read so many awful stories in newspapers about kidnapped children, some kept as prisoners for years, others killed by the sickos who'd run off with them.

"No. No, they never found her. Everyone said that Rebecca was grief stricken, had a nervous breakdown, and never set foot in the hospital again. She left nursing altogether. When the police turned up nothing, Dr. Geringer hired one private detective after another. They tracked down reports of children fitting Stephanie's description all over the country, but none of the leads panned out."

"It must have been horrible for him . . . for both of them," I murmured. Tears dripped between my lashes. I wiped them away. I'd always been a sucker for a sad story, but something made me feel particularly close to Geringer and his pretty wife after hearing this one.

For several minutes I sat very still, silently thinking. "Did Mrs. Geringer leave Chicago to go away for a while? You know, like to recover from losing her little girl?"

"Not that I know of, but anything's possible. I understand she has family on the East Coast."

"No," I muttered, "I haven't been there either."

"You're thinking that you might have seen her, and she frightened you?"

"Yes-s-s," I said slowly. "I must have seen her . . . somewhere in a photo or in real life. . . ."

But the only time I could have seen her in person when she'd behave anything like the woman in my dream was when . . . when Stephanie was being kidnapped and Rebecca ran after the kidnapper, screaming at her to stop.

My brain went into a tailspin. I stared up at Dr. Berman, struggling to catch my breath. "My God . . . oh wow! I think I know where I saw her . . ."

She smiled, looking relieved. "Good for you! Where?"

I slid away from her on the bed. "I . . . I can't say anything yet . . . not until I'm absolutely sure."

thirteen

In my dream, I was being chased by the wild woman again. But this time I used Dr. Berman's dream-spinning technique. She'd said that it would either allow me to control the dream or wake me from it, instead of letting it become an endless chase scene with me as the victim.

I spun and spun with my dream eyes wide open and arms flung apart, feeling cool air whoosh around me. The person who'd been pulling me along and helping me to escape from the wild woman had to let go or be spun with me.

She let go.

She, I thought. *How do I know it's a she?*

I turned and faced the wild woman. It *was* Rebecca Geringer! She was young and pretty. But, as I watched, her face bloated up and turned crimson with fury. She let out a nerve-shredding scream that made me cringe.

"What do you want from me?" I asked.

I didn't shriek out the words in terror. And I didn't try to run from her. I was facing my monster, just as Dr. Berman told me I should, and asking her a simple question.

"Tell me what you want from me," I repeated calmly.

The anger seeped out of Rebecca's features. "Don't you know who I am?" she asked in a sweet voice.

"You are Rebecca . . . Rebecca Geringer."

"No, no . . ." she cooed. "Not Rebecca to you. I'm your—"

"Wake up!" A voice intruded on my dream. "Wake up, Maggie!"

I tried to fight off the interruption. Desperately I spun again, attempting to catch hold of the tattered ends of my dream. For once I didn't want to lose them. I needed to hear what Rebecca was trying to tell me!

"You were dreaming in REM," Dr. Berman said, shaking me. "Tell me exactly what you can recall before it fades."

I pressed my palms over my eyes and groaned. "No! This one's for me. Let me go back to sleep and finish—"

"Finish what?" She still wanted to pump me in the name of science.

"I have to finish finding out who I am."

"You are Maggie Johnson," Dr. Berman said in a clear, sensible voice, but something in her tone hinted at her own doubts.

I let out a disappointed whimper. The dream, nightmare, night terror, vision . . . whatever she wanted to call it, was gone. And so was my link with the past.

I sobbed into my palms. "I almost had it! I was almost there!" I cried.

She patted me softly on the shoulder, then drew me into her arms and rocked me like a little baby.

"No!" I shrieked, fighting her off with my fists.

She jumped away and stared at me. "I was just trying to calm you down after the terrors—"

I cut her off. "It wasn't a terror! I faced the wild woman. It was Rebecca! She was about to tell me something important." The words burst out of me in puffy spurts. I felt as if I'd run miles. I was drenched with sweat.

Dr. Berman sat back down on the edge of the bed and observed me solemnly. "Maggie, haven't I warned you about being overly dramatic? Real life just isn't as weird as you make it out to be," she said gently.

"I'd say that baby stealing is pretty weird." And patient killing was pretty high on my list of strange deeds, too,

I thought. "I have to find out how I know Rebecca," I explained as calmly as I could. "I think she's somehow important to me."

She sighed. "All right. Ask your questions. But keep in mind the people you could hurt just by your nosing around and dredging up the past. You probably just saw her photo somewhere."

"I don't believe that," I said shakily. "I think the dream's been wrong, or at least my interpretation of it has been mixed up from the beginning."

"What do you mean?"

"I-I'm not sure I can explain just yet," I said, popping the electrodes off of my face. I forgot all about my bad arm and started using my right hand as well as my left.

"Maggie! What are you doing?" she gasped.

"I'm through experimenting," I said. "I'm sorry if this ruins your study, Dr. Berman, but I have to do the rest on my own. If I dream, I want to stay there long enough to find answers."

"But the night terrors—" she said, looking concerned. "What if you get pulled into one and you hurt yourself again?"

"I guess I have to take that chance, but I think I can beat them now."

"And if you're wrong?"

"If I'm wrong—" I smiled weakly at her "—I may be in Adolescent Surgery for a long time."

Dr. Berman took away the polygraph, red lamp, yards of wires, and the electrodes. I felt a little bad for spoiling her fun, but worse because she really had helped me by giving me a chance to stay at North Central.

If I hadn't stayed, I might never have stumbled across my own past. And though there were still missing pieces, and the little bit of truth I'd discovered seemed almost too weird to imagine, I felt as if I was on the right track.

Now I had to prove it, not just for myself, but for everyone else.

I had to wait until morning to make the telephone call. When I rang the number that had been left with the desk nurse, my mother answered.

"I was just leaving for work, sweetie. How are you?" she asked.

I swallowed, stopping myself from blurting out the wrong words. "Mom, I need you and Dad to come to the hospital as soon as possible."

"Why? What's wrong?" she asked, instant panic in her voice.

"It's okay, Mom. They just need you both here to release me." I closed my eyes, hating myself for the lie. But there was no other way.

"You can come home now?" she cried. "Oh, that's wonderful!"

"Yeah. When can you guys get here?"

"Oh, well, I don't know," she muttered vaguely. "We have our jobs. And neither of us has been here long enough to ask for a day off." She sounded really nervous. "The drive's too long to make after work and get us back by morning. Maybe just your father could come for you?"

Today is Thursday, I thought. "What about Saturday?" I asked. "Can you both come in two days?"

"I guess that will have to do. Do you think they'll let you stay the extra time? You know . . . without paying?"

"I'm sure it will be okay," I reassured her. "Will you be here Saturday morning?"

"Yes, sometime before noon. Definitely. Oh, I'm so glad you'll be coming home, Maggie. I've missed you so much!"

"Me too, Mom," I choked out, tears filling my eyes.

After I hung up I sat on my bed for a long time and stared at the wall. Two days. I had to wait two whole days to set things right. I didn't know how I was going to fill the time and keep from going crazy.

I shoved up off of the bed, trying to think positive, trying to tell myself that I was doing the right thing and that nothing was more important than the truth. But I wasn't sure anymore. People were going to get hurt.

I had to find Bill. He'd make me feel better. He'd find a way to help me through the next couple of days.

I ran through the corridor, past the breakfast cart. Valerie was helping two nurses pull trays off of it and deliver them to rooms. Her library wagon was parked to the side, with its ink pad and date stamp for checking out books for patients.

I ran past without saying a word to them, even though Valerie shouted a cheery, "Good morning!"

I found Bill in Geriatrics, helping pass out meals. As he disappeared into a room I caught sight of one of the nurses who'd been on duty the day Dr. Geringer had dragged me off the floor and back to my room.

"You'd better get out of here," she warned. "The doctor will be here any minute to check on two of his patients."

"It's okay," I said. "We've made peace, and I won't be long anyway."

A chill slipped across my skin as I approached Mrs. Krane's old room. I couldn't resist peeking inside. An old man lay in the bed she'd died in. He was reading a *Sports Illustrated* magazine.

"Hey there!" Bill called, stepping out of the neighboring room.

"Hey yourself!" I tried to sound happy for the benefit of the nurse who was still watching me. "Mind if I help out?"

"Knock yourself out." He laughed, but his smile teetered when he took a good look at my face. A plastic grin couldn't fool him for long.

"Has something happened?" he asked in an undertone as he checked the meal order taped to the stainless steel dome over a plate.

"Yeah. Something's happened."

"You have more evidence about Mrs. Krane?"

"No," I admitted with a pang of disappointment, "it's not about that."

"What then? You had another night terror?"

"Part of one . . . not enough, though. Dr. Berman woke me up just when something important was about to happen."

"Too bad."

"It's all right, I think. I'm getting close to the end," I said, tension biting into my words. "I'm almost positive I know what caused the terrors to start, and why I haven't shaken them all these years."

"So? What is it?" he asked.

"I . . . I can't really tell you yet," I said. "It wouldn't be fair. I have to tell my family first."

"I understand," he said solemnly. Then after a moment. "If it's real bad and you need someone to be there with you . . ."

"Thanks," I murmured, touching his shoulder. "It is bad . . . the worst. I'd like for you to be there with me. Saturday morning, around eleven o'clock, in my room. There will be a crowd, including Geringer."

He frowned. "Dr. Geringer? What has he got to do with all of this?"

"Without him, I wouldn't be here." I gave him a dim smile. "Come on, these old guys must be starving."

I picked up two covered plates labeled 305A and 305B and walked into the nearest room.

When I came out, Bill was striding into another room across the hall. I could hear him teasing the little old lady in the bed closest to the door about how foxy she looked. She told him she'd had a silver rinse put in her hair the day before. She was getting prettied up to go home.

I grinned. Bill was such a nice guy. Everywhere he went he made people happy. He'd make a great doctor some day.

I grabbed another plate, but a motion at the end of the hall caught my eye. A short, middle-aged man with a

148

red mustache was talking with the nurse. I couldn't hear much of the conversation, but the words "Aunt Adele" floated down the hall toward me.

The nephew, I thought. *That's Mrs. Krane's nephew.*

"Something wrong?" Bill asked, stepping up behind me.

"What's he doing here?" I asked.

"He who?"

"Mrs. Krane's nephew."

"Oh, him. Well, he probably came to pick up her personal stuff."

"No. One of the nurses told me he'd already done that."

"Then I don't know . . ."

As we watched, the man handed the nurse a book with a green-and-white binding. I frowned, wondering why something as simple as a book exchanging hands should send off alarms in my head.

The man quickly left, glancing, as he passed, at the room where his aunt had lived her last days. His eyes dropped away, and he hurried off down the hall.

"If he didn't knock her off, I don't know who did," Bill muttered, clenching his hands at his sides. "He looked guilty as hell."

"Maybe," I murmured, starting to walk down the hall toward the nurse.

I could feel my heart pick up speed the closer I came to her.

"May I see that book?" I asked.

"Oh, hi, Maggie—volunteering today, are you?"

"Sort of." I smiled. "May I look at that for a second?"

"Sure, go ahead," she said, handing the book to me. "In fact, why don't you give it to Valerie when you see her? Mrs. Krane checked it out. Somehow, when the orderly was packing up her personal things, he included it."

"Was that her nephew who just brought it back?"

"Yes, poor guy. I guess the death of a loved one is like that. You think you've put it all behind you, then some little thing pops up to remind you of them. He was nice enough to bring the book back."

"Yes, very nice," I repeated, backing away from her.

I looked down at the cover—*Redford's Guide to Growing Roses*.

Bill peered over my shoulder as the nurse moved off down the hall. "That's interesting."

"What?"

"She must have been planning on doing some gardening."

"Yeah . . ." I whispered hoarsely.

I flipped to the very back, to the pasted-in card with smudged due dates stamped in ink. My finger traced the column down to the final date.

"That's two weeks to the day after she died," Bill murmured.

I closed my eyes, thinking hard. The books were always checked out for exactly two weeks. "But Valerie said she didn't see Mrs. Krane the day she died."

"Maybe she set her date stamp wrong."

"Maybe," I said. There was no reason I could think of for Valerie to lie about having seen her. "I think we should meet with Dr. Geringer."

"Yeah. And we should give him the syringe. It's just too important to leave it unprotected somewhere. If someone found it, they'd throw it away."

I nodded, looking down at the book in my hands. "Roses take a long time to grow. They need a lot of care." Blinking away tears, I gazed up at Bill. "Mrs. K would have wanted to live to see them bloom."

fourteen

Bill and I set off to hunt down Dr. Geringer. We agreed that whoever found him first would take him to the cafeteria and wait there.

While Bill took the elevator to the tenth floor to work down, I started on the first and worked up.

I kept getting a prickly feeling on the back of my neck as I walked down the corridors. It was the kind you get just before you turn around and find someone watching you. But every time I looked behind me, there were only the usual nurses, technicians, and patients. And they all seemed to be going about their normal business. Still, I wanted to get this over with as fast as possible. If we dumped enough evidence in Geringer's lap, he'd have to go to someone—either Mrs. Anderson or the police.

I ran into him in a second-floor waiting room, consulting with another doctor. They were sitting in a sunny corner behind a philodendron plant, talking in hushed voices. When he spotted me, a shadow of irritation flashed across his face. But he cut short his conversation and, after shaking hands with the other doctor, came over to me.

"Can you come to the cafeteria for a cup of coffee?" I asked politely.

"Maggie, that's very nice of you, but I have a lot of patients who need my attention."

"I know," I said, trying to sound calm although my heart was hammering in my chest. "But this is important. I have evidence that someone killed Mrs. Krane."

"Evidence?" he repeated, frowning at me. "We're not talking about theories and guesswork and daydreams. . . ."

"I know what evidence is!"

He sighed. "All right, let's go."

If Bill had been there I would have nailed him with a triumphant *All Right!* look. No matter what other horrors my life held, I was going to catch a murderer. Nothing could bring back Mrs. Krane, but I'd feel better knowing that her killer hadn't gotten away with it and wouldn't kill again.

By the time Bill showed up at the cafeteria, I'd bought three cups of coffee. I flagged him down from a corner table.

"All right, where is this evidence?" Geringer grumbled.

"In a safe place," I said quickly. "The important thing is, we *know* that someone killed Mrs. Krane, and probably several other patients the same way."

"Who?"

"There are several possibilities for the police to look into. Her nephew is one, another is Valerie Tucker."

"The volunteer in charge of the library wagon?" Geringer rolled his eyes in exasperation. He started to stand up. "Come on, kids, this isn't a game—"

My hand shot out, grabbing the sleeve of his white jacket. "She had access to all the patients' rooms! She *lied* to me, said she hadn't seen Mrs. Krane the day she died, but she did because she stamped her book that day. She—"

Geringer shook off my grip. "Maybe she just forgot. Have you thought of that?" He turned to Bill. "I'm surprised at you, son. This young lady obviously has a pretty active imagination, but you've always seemed like a level-headed young man to me."

"Yes, sir," Bill said shakily. "But if you'll please just listen for a minute. There really are enough suspicious things happening to deserve some kind of investigation."

Geringer threw up his hands. "This is preposterous! We've already discussed the nephew. He has no motive for killing other patients, and Mrs. Krane had no money to leave him. And why in God's name would a teenage volunteer want to kill anyone? These people were all strangers to her! Most were short-term patients. She couldn't possibly have gotten to know them very well."

"Maybe they were mercy killings . . . she felt sorry for them," Bill suggested.

"No," Geringer stated emphatically, standing up. "With the exception of Gregory Brown, an eighty-year-old man with terminal lung cancer, they were all scheduled to leave here and would be able to live fairly comfortable lives. None of them was in terrible pain. We're not talking lingering death throes here."

I shot to my feet before he could leave. "Please!" I cried. "Please wait. I found a used syringe under Mrs. Krane's bed. It has traces of insulin in it. We had it analyzed, so we know. There might have been enough in the syringe to kill her."

Geringer looked as if he were listening for the first time. "I didn't prescribe insulin for her. . . ."

"Yes, sir. We know," Bill said quietly.

Geringer chewed his bottom lip, glancing around the cafeteria uneasily, then quickly sat down, "It's not much, but if there are fingerprints on the syringe . . ."

"They're probably gone by now," I admitted reluctantly. "Both Bill and I handled it, and then there was the lab tech."

The doctor let out an exasperated grunt. "All right, where is this syringe?"

"Like I said, in a safe place."

"Get it for me, and I'll take it to the police right now. We won't wait for Mrs. Anderson."

I threw my arms around him, and he tensed up all over. Probably not too many teenage girls hugged him. Stepping back, I grinned at him bashfully.

"Want me to go with you to get it?" Bill asked.

I shook my head. "No. I'll be right back. It should only take ten minutes."

I ran down the hall to the elevator and took it to the eighth floor. This time of the morning, the public areas were crowded with newly admitted patients, lab techs making their rounds to draw blood for tests, orderlies pushing wheelchairs for patients on their way to X ray, and nurses and doctors carrying cups of coffee to their work areas.

I looked around uneasily. The nerve-teasing feeling that I was being followed returned. But no one at all threatening-looking was in sight.

I was glad now that I'd been so careful about hiding the syringe. Its appearance under Mrs. K's bed might be just questionable enough to bring in the police. It might be the key to a half dozen murders!

I hurried down the hall, excited because we were so close to the end of our hunt. Pushing between people who were walking too slowly, I ran all the way to the end of the old wing, to where the new construction started. When I came to the plastic curtain, I peeked through.

Although the noise from riveting and drilling equipment was almost deafening, none of the workmen seemed to be on the eighth floor.

I glanced behind me to make sure no one was watching. If a security guard saw me, he'd stop me from entering the work area. For a second I thought I glimpsed a motion just around the first corner, but nothing appeared. With a dull, ticklish feeling in my stomach that I couldn't explain, I stepped cautiously onto the bare cement slab in the new wing and held my breath. I felt as if I were testing a pond for skating, wondering if the ice would hold me on a mild January day.

Slowly I moved forward, over the concrete floor that led past the crude construction elevator.

As I eased past the open shaft of the elevator, I looked down the narrow metal cavity. Far below was the roof of the passenger compartment, and that seemed to be where most of the noise was coming from—the first or second floor.

Excitement bubbled up in my throat as I approached the cluster of pipes where I'd hidden the syringe. Kneeling on the raw cement floor cluttered with masonry chips, bits of wire, and construction dust, I reached into the open end of the drainpipe and felt around.

"S-s-s-o that's where you put it," a voice hissed.

I snapped around, my heart plummeting into the pit of my stomach. Valerie stood above me.

Her hands were braced on her wide hips, and her eyes were black and menacing. She was wearing her pink-and-white candy-striper smock and her smily-face badge. But she wasn't smiling.

I pulled my hand free, leaving behind the plastic sack my fingertips had brushed, and started to stand up.

"No, no . . . go right ahead," she said with eerie politeness. "Pull it out. Let me see what you've got."

"Nothing's there. One of the workmen must have found it and thrown—"

"Cut the crap, Maggie!" she growled. "You're a lousy liar."

Still half-crouching, I backed away.

"Don't!" she shouted, her voice barely carrying above the whine of power equipment from below. "You pull that syringe out of there and hand it to me, right now!"

Something in the fierceness of her tone warned me that I shouldn't refuse her.

I tried one last bluff. "I don't know what you're talking about."

"I heard you and Bill talking," she snapped coldly. "I was in a patient's room right behind you two when you were looking at Mrs. Krane's book. You two thought you could trap me. But it won't work."

"Oh, no?" I could be sly, too. "Well, Bill's with Dr. Geringer in the cafeteria right this minute. We've already told him about the lethal dose of insulin you injected into Mrs. Krane."

Her glare wavered, and for a moment she looked worried. "But he doesn't have the syringe, and that's what counts." She chuckled. "Hey, girl, all the police have to go on is what you tell them. No one in this hospital believes a thing Maggie Johnson says. Why should the cops? Even Dr. Berman thinks you are totally brain-scrambled."

"She doesn't!"

"Oh, yes she does. Berman humors you so she can keep you in her research project. She doesn't care whether you ever stop having your nightmares and delusions—you're a valuable and rare little guinea pig. And Geringer, well, he's a hopeless case. People tolerate his pompous rages because they feel sorry for him, for what happened to him and his wife."

My stomach started to cramp up with fear. "No," I whispered. "People will listen."

Valerie shook her head. "No, they won't." She started moving toward me. "They won't listen, because there won't be anyone to listen to."

I backed away from her. "You're going to kill me, too?"

"Yes," she said calmly.

"Why kill me if everyone thinks I'm loony?" I asked.

"Insurance. Who knows, one of these days maybe you'll get a grip on things and people will start paying attention to you."

A horrible thought struck me. "You're not just worried about the police finding out about Mrs. Krane and people you killed before her, are you? You're planning on murdering more patients!"

She grinned. "It's the perfect business."

"Business?" I croaked out, horrified.

She stepped forward, tucking the plastic-wrapped syringe into her smock pocket. "The first one, I just felt sorry for," Valerie explained. "He was a real old

156

guy. Man, what a mess. He couldn't eat by himself or go to the bathroom like a normal person. Everything went into him and out of him through tubes."

"But he was *alive!*" I shouted.

"Yeah, sure, if you call that living." She shook her head, chuckling to herself again. The noise from below had gotten so loud, she didn't seem worried that anyone might have had heard me. "My grandmother is diabetic. I give her insulin injections when she needs them. I know how to do it, and how important it is for her. But she told me once that if she got too much, she could go into shock and die."

"You used her medicine?"

Valerie looked pleased with herself. "One time I told her I'd lost her prescription on the way to the drugstore. But I filled it and kept it. Another time I called the druggist for a refill when she didn't really need one. It wasn't hard to stockpile enough of the stuff for when I needed it."

"But you *killed* people who were getting better! Mrs. Krane might have lived happily for years!"

Valerie sighed. "It didn't matter anymore. After I injected the first guy, I felt a little guilty. I mean, I knew I'd done the right thing for *him*. He'd really been in awful shape; he was helpless. But I felt sorry for his family, until I heard his son and daughter talking."

"What did they say?" I breathed.

I was only half-listening to her by now. My brain was scrambling for possible ways to save myself. I scanned the rough floor for a tool a workman might have left behind—anything I could use to defend myself.

"His family?" she repeated distantly. "Oh, they looked a little teary-eyed, but mostly they kept saying that it was probably for the best he'd gone when he did. His medical care was so expensive, they didn't know how much longer they could have paid the bills before they ran out of money."

"I don't get it," I said, although I was beginning to . . . I just needed to buy time. Maybe Bill would get impatient when I didn't show up, and he'd come looking for me.

"You really are dense!" Valerie snapped. "Listen, sick people's relatives need help, too. They're glad to pay a final thousand dollars to end all the hospital and doctors' bills before they get snowed under by debt."

"So you started an elimination business?" I murmured, still unwilling to believe anyone could be so wicked and cold.

Valerie's doughy face split into a smile. "Exactly. All I had to do was listen in on visitors' conversations. They never thought about my being in the room with my book cart; they just yapped away. If they expressed concern over finances or fear of their relatives suffering, I tuned in."

"Then you walked right up to them and said, 'Hey, want me to bump off Nana for you?' "

"Of course not!" she snapped disdainfully. "Give me credit for a little sensitivity. I got the nearest relation's phone number from the patient's chart. Then I'd call him at home. Of course he'd never know who I was, so he couldn't turn me in if he'd wanted to. But none of them wanted to. I promised to help their loved ones go gently to sleep one more time . . . and never wake up again. The patients would be out of pain, and there would be no more worries about money or how to care for them . . . All the family had to do was refuse an autopsy and arrange for cremation the next day."

"Nice and tidy—no evidence," I commented drily.

"Right."

She'd backed me up along the cement walkway. The curtain separating the new and old buildings blew gently back and forth in the chill wind off Lake Michigan. Hopefully, my glance flickered toward it, but Valerie must have sensed my intention to make a mad dash for safety. She quickly maneuvered around me to block my path.

"You're not leaving that way," she said.

"No? Maybe I'm not, but you'd better get out of here pretty fast. Bill and Geringer will come looking for me any minute. They know where I am."

She shrugged. "We'll both be gone in a few minutes." With a cunning twinkle in her eye, she drew a small syringe from her smock pocket and removed the plastic shield from its needle.

"What's that for?" I asked, terror rippling through my veins, because I could guess.

"A sedative. I picked it up off a nurse's medication tray."

She was going to drug me. I'd be helpless to fight her or run away then.

"Maybe the visions in your poor demented mind are too much for you to deal with?" she mused. "Maybe you started snitching drugs to get high. Then you just happened to stumble into a dangerous part of the construction. A lot of accidents can happen in a place like this. . . ."

"Valerie, no!" I choked out. "You'll get caught sooner or later, if not for killing me then for killing those poor old people."

"I don't think so," she said. "I'm pretty careful."

The tip of the needle glittered with a drop of dangerous golden liquid. Without warning, she lunged for me.

fifteen

I threw myself to one side, but Valerie caught hold of my left wrist with her free hand. Her grip was like rock. No matter how hard I twisted or pulled, I couldn't break free.

"Let go!" I screamed.

With my right arm still strapped to my chest, I couldn't pry her fingers loose. I jerked hard, but only managed to knock her off balance. She fell to the hard cement floor, dragging me down with her.

She must have outweighed me by at least thirty pounds. Rolling over on top of me, Valerie pinned my wrists with her big hand to my chest.

Desperately I thrashed my legs around, trying to keep her too busy to aim accurately at a vein in my arm.

"Hold still!" she grunted, moving the needle closer. "You don't want the needle to break off under your skin, do you? That would really hurt!"

Like dying won't? I thought wildly.

"Let me go!" I shrieked. Wrenching my head around, I stared helplessly toward the plastic curtain. How long had I been gone? I'd told Bill ten minutes. It must have been longer than that already. *Please come looking for me! Please!* I prayed silently.

"You might as well quit fighting me," Valerie said breathlessly. "I'm a lot stronger than you, and I'm not going to let you ruin the best job I've ever had."

I stared up into her eyes. They were as emotionless

160

as stones. At that moment, it hit me that she had no idea of right or wrong. Maybe before her first murder, she'd understood. But no longer. The only survival that now meant anything to Valerie was her own.

I fought to push her off, but it was no use. She was right, she was stronger. After a few more minutes I was exhausted by the struggle, and the pain that roared through my injured shoulder had become unbearable.

I watched in horror as she slowly lowered the needle's point and plunged it into my arm. Depressing the syringe, she released the pale yellow fluid into my blood stream.

"No-o-o-o!" I wailed.

She sat on top of me for a while longer, catching her breath, keeping my fists pinned against my heaving chest, watching my face for signs of the drug beginning to work.

It kicked in quickly.

I felt a pleasant warmth and numbness slip through my limbs, and my head began to spin. It was sort of like the time I'd experimented with a jug of Gallo at a party and wound up getting sick all over the couch. I'd never done it again.

I blinked my heavy, heavy eyelids, gazing up at Valerie's blurry features. Her satisfied smile looked almost friendly now. I felt her release me and climb off.

"I can breathe now," I said thankfully.

"Yeah, but not for long," she muttered. "Come on. Get up."

"Don't feel like it," I mumbled, rolling over onto my side and curling up in a cozy fetal position. In the back of my mind I knew what she wanted to do. She wanted to kill me. But all I cared about was going to sleep.

"Yer worryin' 'bout nothin'," I slurred.

"Huh?" Valerie grunted.

She was trying to hoist me up under my arms into a

standing position. It wasn't that I didn't want to cooperate. My legs were rubbery and refused to support me. I kept crumbling to the floor.

"I didn't think you were this heavy a minute ago," she groaned.

"Heavy . . . heavy . . . heavy . . ." I chanted dreamily, drawing patterns in the dust on the cement with my index finger. The last one was a heart. I wrote "Bill" in the center.

"Good grief!" she muttered. "I should have either given you less of that stuff, or enough to knock you out for good!"

I glanced up and saw three Valeries standing over me with a look of disgust on their faces, fists propped on hips as they considered what to do with troublesome little me.

"Sorry," I sang out, "can't get up . . . just can't do it . . ."

"Well, there's a way around anything," she ground out with determination.

Seizing my feet, she started dragging me across the floor toward the elevator shaft. *So this is where she wanted me all along,* a corner of my brain churned out. *But I don't want to go in there, do I? It's kind of a long way down. . . .*

Maybe the instinct to survive is stronger than any chemical that can be pumped into a person's body. Or maybe Valerie was right, she just hadn't gotten the dose right. Whatever the reason, I sensed that I couldn't let her dump me into that shaft. I'd never survive an eight-story drop.

But the dusty floor made it easy for her to slide me backward on my belly toward the elevator. I reached out, scrambling for something to hold onto, something to stop the awful progress toward the long drop to my death. But she was careful to keep me away from the strong steel girders that would someday support walls.

We reached the elevator shaft, and Valerie stopped,

still holding my ankles. She seemed to be having trouble figuring out how to drag me over the edge without getting too close to the opening herself.

" 'Fraid of heights?" I asked.

"Shut up!" she snapped. Dropping my legs near the hole, she quickly stepped around in front of me to push the rest of my body closer to the shaft. I reached out and caught hold of her big white nurse's shoe.

"Knock it off!" she shouted. "Being stubborn won't do you any good!"

"If I have to go down there," I said in a surprisingly rational voice, "you're going with me. At least then you can't kill anyone else."

"Give me a break!" she laughed, kicking her leg violently to loosen my grasp.

Something told me this was my very last chance. If she once broke my grip, all she had to do was give me one good push in the chest and my body weight would carry me over the edge.

I held on for my life. Held on and screamed at the top of my lungs—hoping that, by some miracle, all the drills and saws and jackhammers would quit for just a second, and someone would hear me.

As Valerie swung her leg back and forth, trying to loosen my fingers, my head flopped from side to side, banging against the cement floor. My shoulder had passed simple pain and moved on to agony, and my ribs burned like fire. Somehow I managed to grab her other foot, which threw her off balance. She fell on top of me, and we rolled over a couple of times until our legs ended up kicking air over the elevator shaft.

"You stupid little witch!" she cried. "You're going to die whether you like it or not!"

"I know," I ground out between clenched teeth, "but so are you!"

Clinging to her, I started inching backward, toward the hole, instead of fighting her. Because her legs were dangling free, she couldn't get any traction and her big body slid farther and farther into the deep, dark shaft with mine.

Her eyes flew wide open, staring at me in shock. "You're crazy!" She let out a long, piercing scream that made mine seem like baby chick peeps.

Yanking on her uniform, I wedged my knees against a metal girder to move us farther over the edge. Valerie fought to pry my fingers away from her clothing, then flailed her arms wildly, hitting me in the face while grappling for a girder of her own. But she was at a bad angle to grab hold of anything, and gravity was in my favor.

I felt the last of my strength finally seep out of me. "It's almost over," I whispered. "Then I'll sleep. . . . No night terrors . . . no waking up in cold sweats . . . just the sleep of the dead . . ."

I closed my eyes, releasing Valerie's smock and blocking out her hysterical scrambling and shrieks. She must have found something to hold onto at the last minute, because she was still making awful noises. I didn't care anymore. I'd done all I could do.

Resting my head on the steel framing, I closed my eyes and sniffed cement dust and machine oil into my nostrils. I clung limply to a thin cable as my hips slipped farther over the lip of the shaft. I couldn't be sure the cable was attached to anything, but it seemed better than holding onto nothing as I went over the edge. I wasn't afraid to die, now that there was nothing I could do about it. I drifted deeper toward unconsciousness.

Suddenly I felt something rush past me, and the noise of Valerie's screams stopped. I slipped another two inches over the edge and prayed I'd already be dead before I hit bottom. I didn't want to be able to feel anything when my body smashed into the pavement eight floors down.

Then, as if from a great distance, I heard voices. Someone forced my fingers open, and I came halfway out of my drugged daze to cry, "No! No, if I let go I'll fall!"

"I won't let you fall," a deep male voice promised.

I didn't care who it was, just as long as it wasn't Valerie, still trying to trick me.

"Okay," I mumbled, too exhausted to open my eyes. And I let go.

I don't know how long it took for the stuff Valerie had injected me with to wash out of my bloodstream. But when it did, I woke up for a few minutes and looked around.

Somehow I'd expected to see angels, or at least my parents leaning over my deathbed. Instead, there was Dr. Geringer, sitting in a chair in a corner of the room, reading a chart with his glasses halfway down his long nose. I closed my eyes and drifted off again.

It was the next day before I really woke up. This time only a nurse was in the room, sitting where Geringer had been and flipping through a magazine.

"You're awake," she said brightly.

"I guess," I murmured. Being awake didn't seem so remarkable. Being *alive* was the real point.

My right arm was wrapped close to my chest again, and I could feel surgical tape pulling at the flesh around my shoulder and ribs. I lifted my left hand to my head and touched it, feeling for bandages, casts, anything that would indicate I'd fallen eight stories and somehow lived to tell the tale.

When nothing turned up in the penthouse, my fingers quickly traveled toward the basement—my arms . . . ribs . . . thighs . . .

"You're all there, if that's what you're wondering," the nurse said, smiling.

"Good," I said, "that's good."

There was a glass of water on the table by the bed. I reached for it. She beat me to it and helped me take slow sips.

I was relieved to see no one had hooked me up to tubes or monitors. That seemed to be another happy sign.

"What happened?" I asked.

"You'd better talk to Dr. Geringer about that," she said, getting up out of her chair. "I'll call him." She was almost to the door when she turned back. "Oh, maybe you should know that the police have been waiting to talk to you. The doctor sent them away for the time being, but I guess they'll want some information from you soon."

It couldn't have been more than five minutes before Geringer burst into the room. He looked as if he'd been running—his graying hair mussed, eyes dilated, breathing labored and raspy.

He stopped just inside the door as soon as he saw me looking at him. "Well, you don't look all that bad, considering," he said, suddenly looking sheepish.

"No thanks to you," I grumbled.

"What?"

"If you'd believed me from the beginning, I wouldn't have had to wrestle a crazy candy striper."

He shook his head. "I'm sorry, Maggie. I really wanted to believe you. I had my own suspicions, but I'd never have thought that girl was killing patients. She had no obvious motive. . . ."

I shrugged, and a streak of pain shot through my shoulder. "Ow!" I cried.

"It's not surprising you reinjured that collarbone," he said, coming over to prod me with his gentle fingers.

"What about Valerie?" I asked, holding my breath. I had to know.

"She's going to be all right, at least physically," he said.

"She is?"

"Your friend Bill and I came looking for you when you didn't return to the cafeteria. I thought you'd just decided not to come back when I'd called your bluff by asking to see the evidence. But Bill insisted that something had to be wrong."

"Good old Bill," I murmured fondly. "He was the only one who took me seriously."

166

"Well, you won't have that trouble anymore."

I looked up at Geringer and saw something startlingly familiar in his eyes. But then that shouldn't have been surprising, knowing what I now knew about my past . . . and about his Stephanie.

But there would be time to talk about that later.

"How did Valerie survive a fall like that? I thought I felt her drop past me."

He nodded. "You were both inches from oblivion when we reached the elevator. I grabbed for you at the same time Bill hit the elevator button. Valerie fell before he could get his hands on her, but by then the passenger cage had reached somewhere around the sixth floor. She might have dropped twenty feet, a bad enough fall to break her leg but certainly not enough to kill her."

I frowned.

"Don't worry. She can't come after you again," he said, reading my mind. "She's being held in police custody until she's well enough to be moved to a regular jail cell. She'll be tried for the murder of Mrs. Krane and possibly four other patients."

"You mean, the syringe really was enough evidence?" I murmured.

"Not really," Geringer said. "Valerie was so shaken by the fall, she broke down and confessed to administering lethal doses of insulin to each of the victims. The police are working on getting statements out of their relatives who hired her. But so far no one's admitting a thing."

I shook my head. "I still can't believe it. Killing a person to save a few dollars."

A knock sounded on the door.

"Come in," I said automatically.

Bill poked his head around the doorway. "I got word through the grapevine you were awake."

"Yeah, Dr. Geringer was just telling me what a great job of button pushing you did," I teased.

He blushed. "Not exactly a superhero's feat, huh?"

I smiled at him. "Sometimes you have to do what makes sense at the time." I was thinking of my decision to take Valerie with me down the elevator shaft. I shivered, realizing how close I'd come to the end of my life.

Dr. Geringer coughed softly. Glancing up, I saw him watching me with a curiously sad look in his eyes. "I have to go now," he said abruptly.

"You'll be here tomorrow when my parents come?" I asked.

"Maybe we should say good-bye now," he said softly. "I'm even worse at good-byes than I am at hellos."

I grinned, remembering the way he'd roared at me for daring to hang out with his patient. "No," I said firmly, "you have to be here. I won't leave until you come."

Geringer looked puzzled. "All right, if you insist. Eleven o'clock?"

"Yes," I said, "eleven."

As soon as Geringer closed the door behind him, Bill pounced on me. "What the heck was that all about?"

"If you don't know, I'm not going to tell you."

"I hate when girls say that!" he groaned.

I giggled. "Don't look so stressed out. I'm the one whose life is about to get crazy."

"Crazier than it's already been?" he asked.

" 'Fraid. so."

He leaned over and kissed me on the lips. "I think maybe some of Val's drug dripped into your brain."

sixteen

"You look like a caged lioness," Bill remarked when I crossed to my hospital room window and peered out at the parking lot for the hundredth time that morning.

"I can't help it," I said. "They'll be here soon."

But the hours had seemed to crawl past. I couldn't read, watch TV, or eat. I was so nervous I hadn't sat down since eight o'clock that morning.

Bill sat quietly, watching me pace. At last he interrupted our silence. "I'm going to miss you, Maggie."

I turned to face him, for a minute confused. My head had been elsewhere, trying out words . . . the words that would shock everyone in the room, except Dr. Berman and me, because we knew the truth. For the sake of that truth I was going to turn all of our lives upside down, again.

"I'll see you somehow," was all I could say for now.

"Yeah, right." Bill let out a low, unhappy chuckle and scuffed at the floor with his Adidas. "You'll be somewhere in Ohio, and I'll be here in Chicago. But maybe you're right. Maybe we'll find ways to see each other. I think we could be pretty super together, Maggie."

I grinned at him. "I know we could."

"Knock knock!" came a cheerful voice from the doorway.

"Hey, Doc!" Bill crowed. "You here for the big send-off?"

Dr. Berman looked at me with a concerned expression. "Are you sure you want to do this, Maggie?"

"I have to. You know I do," I said softly.

She smiled at me. "I suppose so."

"Will someone tell me what's going on!" Bill pleaded.

But halting footsteps approached the door, and the three of us turned to face their owners.

Francine and Carl stood in the doorway, peering inside cautiously. I don't know when I'd started thinking of them by their first names, but it seemed the natural thing to do. Now that I knew the secret they'd held onto for twelve long years.

"Are you almost ready?" Carl asked. "We have to get back home real quick. My boss offered me overtime work tonight."

"We're almost ready," I said, avoiding the issue of home.

"Are you packed?" Francine asked, swinging her red curls around to eye my open suitcase on the bed.

"No. I wanted to talk to you first."

She scowled at me, then shot her husband a nervous look.

"Let's get going, young lady," he said gruffly. "No more stalling. The doc has had plenty of time to dig around in your head. If she hasn't come up with anything about your dreams by now, she isn't going to."

I bit down on my lower lip and stared at my watch, hoping Dr. Geringer was on his way.

"I don't know why the hospital had to make both of us come for you." Francine whimpered. "I told you your dad would come. Why both of us?"

Her voice rose higher and higher with every word. She wrung her hands and licked her lips anxiously, glancing toward Dr. Berman as if hopeful that medical science would agree unreasonable demands had been placed on her.

"I think Maggie wants us all here for a special reason,"

170

a deep voice spoke up from the doorway. "Although, like you, I'm not exactly sure what that is."

Carl and Francine spun around and stared at Geringer.

"Who the hell are you? Another one of these crackpot physicians?" Carl demanded. "Listen, I've had about enough of you folks. I'm taking my daughter home with me, and there isn't a thing you can do about it."

"That's what you wanted to do from the minute the ambulance brought me here, isn't it?" I asked quietly.

Carl turned to me, a frantic expression slowly seeping over the anger in his eyes. "Of course it is. I never trusted hospitals and doctors. You read about god-awful things that happen in places like this. Just this morning, I heard on the radio 'bout those old folks who got offed by some crazy volunteer."

The story of Valerie's ghoulish "business" had apparently already hit the news.

"But other things happen that aren't very pleasant—right, Mr. Johnson?" Dr. Berman demanded, her eyes growing stormy.

For a moment, the room was silent. So deathly silent, I couldn't even hear myself breathing.

At last Carl grumbled, "Get your suitcase, Maggie. Let's get out of here."

"No." I stood straightened up and met his eyes. "I don't think I belong with you."

Francine threw herself across the room at me. "Of course you belong with us! What's the matter with you? You're our little girl . . . our little Maggie!" she shrieked at the top of her lungs, squashing my cheeks between her palms.

"No," I said firmly, stepping back from her. "I'm not Maggie, and I've never been yours."

Carl turned on Dr. Berman. "See what you've done to this girl!" he shouted. "You brainwashed her. You turned her against her own parents!"

But beneath his anger I glimpsed the same look of fear I'd seen in his eyes every time he'd taken me to

171

an emergency room after a violent night terror. The same fear that was there just before we rushed out of one town, heading for another.

"I don't brainwash my patients," Dr. Berman stated coldly.

Dr. Geringer took a deep breath and looked at me. "Maggie, I don't know what's going on here, and I think your parents are very confused, too. But this time they are right about one thing—they can take you home. Dr. Winschel told me there's been no internal bleeding, and you seem to feel that Dr. Berman can't help you any more."

"They aren't my parents," I said.

Geringer let out a strangled sound and swerved around to stare at Francine and Carl. "What?"

Bill was watching me with more interest than shock. Dr. Berman just looked intrigued with how everyone was reacting to the news that she'd figured out for herself.

"I think everyone should sit down now and listen to what I have to say," I told them.

"I'm not staying for any more of this nonsense," Carl growled at no one in particular. "The girl has been borderline nuts for years. She doesn't know what she's saying!" He grabbed his wife by the wrist and marched her toward the door.

Geringer stepped to one side to block the doorway. "If you try to leave before Maggie's finished, I'll call the police," he threatened.

Carl glared at him but didn't force his way past. Francine gave me a pitiful look and collapsed into the nearest chair, dropping her face into her hands with a moan. She must have figured out that I knew what she'd done. The crime she'd committed had caught up with her at last, and nothing her husband did or said now could save her.

I turned toward Geringer, and his gray eyes locked on mine. "I'm Stephanie. I'm Stephanie Geringer, your daughter," I said in a strong, clear voice.

Tears pooled in his eyes at the mention of her name . . . *my* name. But he didn't move toward me. Unable to speak, he shook his head slowly in denial.

"You!" Bill gasped. "You were the little girl who was kidnapped from this hospital?"

"Yes," I murmured. "I guess I must have always known, somewhere in the very back of my mind, that I didn't belong with the two people who called themselves my parents." I turned to face them. "I mean, it wasn't like you treated me horribly. You were as good to me as if I was your own real daughter. You loved me, I could tell that. And I loved . . ." I choked once but plunged on. "I still love you! You did everything you could for me. You even spent twelve years running from the police to keep me."

Francine sobbed loudly into her hands. Her cries filled the room.

Carl dropped his hand to her shoulder. "You shouldn't do this to her. She doesn't deserve it, Maggie. She loves you so much."

"But it's the truth!" I insisted. "And the truth is important!"

He didn't try to argue that.

I went on. "The thing is, my subconscious must have remembered the day she took me from the waiting room. It must have been the most frightening day of my three-year-old life. It stayed with me, in my dreams. I saw the hospital corridors, these very same ones, and I sensed I was being pulled along."

"But you had the explanations all wrong," Dr. Berman whispered. "You thought the woman chasing you wanted to hurt you and the person who was pulling you along by your hand was trying to help you escape from her."

"Right," I said, the old sick fear tickling at my gut. "I didn't know that the wild woman in my terrors was my *real* mother, and she wasn't screaming at *me* to stop. . . . She wasn't screaming that she'd kill *me*. . . . She was threatening to kill my kidnapper if the woman didn't let me go."

"You recognized Rebecca from the photo on my desk," Geringer murmured, his face ashen. "That's why you were so upset that day in my office. Oh my God, you *are* Stephanie!"

I looked at the couple who had pretended to be my parents for almost as far back as my memory would take me. The woman looked like a stranger to me, shriveled up in the orange vinyl chair beside the hospital bed. The man simply stared at me.

At last Carl said, "It's a long time past, Maggie. Water under the bridge." He licked his lips, chancing a glance at Geringer. "We're tired of running. There's no use pretending that she's ours. I guess there are scientific ways, tests and things that could prove we're not related."

Geringer nodded stiffly.

Carl turned back to me. "But blood isn't so important. You love us, don't you, Maggie? We raised you. You're more a part of us than you are of him." He pointed a shaky finger at Geringer. "I'll bet a stuffed shirt like that doesn't even know how to have fun with a kid."

Geringer lurched forward, his fists clenched. "*I never had a chance to have fun with my little girl!*" he roared. "I was robbed of the most precious gift of my life, you bastard! My wife and I never gave up trying to find our child, never gave up hoping she might be alive . . . somewhere."

Carl dropped back a step, as if afraid Geringer was going to attack him. "I . . . I didn't have anything to do with it. Francie just wanted a baby so bad, and she couldn't have one of her own. We tried. We tried for years. Then one day—" He shot a worried look at his wife, but she just sat in a limp ball, staring at the floor. "—One day, something just snapped inside of her. I came home from work and found her playing with this little kid like she was a doll. She'd dressed her up in a frilly pink dress with white bows in her hair. Francie was so happy. I'd never seen her that happy as long as I'd known her."

174

"You *knew* she'd kidnapped the child," Dr. Berman stated, "and you didn't go to the police."

"Yeah. Yeah, of course I knew it. I tried for days to make her see she should take the kid back, but she wouldn't."

"So we spent the next dozen years running," I said.

"Because we loved you, Maggie," Carl whispered.

Maggie? I thought. *No, not Maggie. I'm Stephanie Geringer, and I'd better get used to the name*. It was mine and, whether or not the Geringers wanted me, I was going to use it.

"At first, the Johnsons must have been running from the police," Dr. Berman explained solemnly. "But after a time, when the police detectives hit nothing but dead ends, they must have stopped investigating the case."

"Yes," Geringer choked out. "They told us that chances were, Stephanie was dead."

He blinked away tears before going on. "I hired private detectives. When one found nothing new, I dropped him and hired another one. Sometimes they thought they'd found a little girl who might be our daughter, but before they could get to her, she'd disappear." He kept glancing at me, as if afraid I'd vanish in a puff of smoke any second. "It might have been you, Maggie. Or it might have been a false lead. There were plenty of those, too," he said sadly.

No wonder the Stephanie file was so thick, I thought.

I couldn't take my eyes off of his face. It was broader and sharper than mine—the nose long, the mouth a little downturned at the corners. But otherwise, *it was my face*! Why hadn't I seen myself in him before?

But I guess we see what we want to in people. And I'd decided from the start that Geringer was nothing more than an arrogant doctor who didn't care about his patients.

I smiled at how wrong I'd been.

"What are you thinking, Mag—" Geringer cleared his throat. "That is, *Stephanie* . . . what are you thinking?"

I liked the sound of my name. It felt special and right to my ears.

"I was just wondering about how twisted a person's mind can get." I glanced at Francine.

As emotionally messed up as I'd been, she must have been ten times worse. No wonder she was always a nervous wreck. It was more than just the thought of losing me. She and Carl must have become terrified of getting caught and being sent away to prison for kidnapping. They probably stole my mail and intercepted phone calls from my old friends, making sure the ties were cut between moves. That way they couldn't tip off the private detectives the Geringers had hired. But they didn't know what to do with *me*. It's not like they could just give me back and say, "Sorry."

I shook my head, wondering what was going to happen next. I didn't have a home anymore, and my old parents weren't really my parents at all. I couldn't go with them now. But Geringer and his wife were strangers. I mean, let's get real here, you don't just pop up on someone's doorstep as a teenager and say, "Hey, guys! Guess what? I'm your long-lost daughter, where's my bedroom?"

I felt Bill's arm come around me as tears trickled down my cheeks.

It was several hours later when Dr. Geringer returned to my hospital room. Bill was still with me, but the police had come and taken the Johnsons away. Dr. Berman had left after promising to stop by once she'd seen her other patients.

"I've brought a visitor," he said, gesturing to someone outside in the hall. A woman with soft silver streaks in her dark hair stepped into the room and moved into his arms. She was crying, but every now and then she'd crack open one eye and peek at me.

She looked a lot older than she had in the photograph of the three of us, and not at all scary like the wild woman in my terrors. But it was her. Rebecca Geringer. My mother.

Bill nudged me. "You'd better go to her," he whispered in my ear.

"I . . . I can't," I stammered. *What if she didn't want me? What if she blamed me for leaving her?*

But something in the way Geringer gazed over her head at me beckoned me forward.

Suddenly I was rushing across the room, streaking across the years of confusion and fear and unknowing heartache into their arms. My mother turned at the touch of my hand on her back and crushed me against her, sobbing into my hair and stroking the back of my head as a flood of tears washed down her face.

"My darling . . . my darling Stephie," she cried.

"It's okay. I'm here. I'm back now," was all I could think to say.

She pushed me abruptly away from her and studied my face through red eyes. "Oh, my!" she breathed. "You're even more beautiful than I'd imagined you'd turn out. Please forgive me, forgive me for not coming for you."

I laughed out loud, suddenly too happy for any more tears. "Forgive you? You couldn't help what happened. It wasn't your fault."

"I never should have left you in that waiting room. Never, never should have . . . but you're here. Now you're here."

I was aware of other people in the room, but only as shadows. It was as if they'd faded away, unimportant at this moment. There was only *her*—my mother—and me. I could feel her love closing softly around me. A love so strong that she'd never given up hope.

She must have read something of my thoughts. "They kept telling us they'd found you," she sobbed. "Some detective would come to us with a new lead, saying he'd found you in a foster home, or with some cult in California, or living on the street with a group of drugged-out kids. We'd fly across the country, but it wasn't you, of course. Every time I prayed it would be you. Every time my heart broke when it wasn't."

Then I knew where my home was, and I knew I'd be welcome there. My life felt as if it fit me for the first time ever.

seventeen

It was my sixteenth birthday, and I was allowed to invite six friends to spend the night at our house overlooking Lake Michigan. Elly was the first name that came to mind. Rebecca and I talked about her coming to visit, and she'd suggested Elly stay for at least a week.

Slowly, I'd gotten used to the place again. Little snatches of memory told me that the room I'd been given had once been a nursery—mine. Rebecca had turned it into a sewing and reading room after I'd been gone for seven years. My dad had convinced her it wasn't healthy to keep it decorated as a baby's room, since it seemed I wasn't coming back.

But she'd kept my dolls and stuffed animals. They'd been given a place of honor on a narrow white shelf above her sewing machine.

Rebecca and I had spent a whole month redecorating the room with fresh wallpaper and paint, buying furniture, sewing curtains. It was a beautiful bedroom—a cool mint green with white trim around the doors and windows, and touches of deep pink in the bedspread and sheets. A thick white rug spread across the polished wood floor. My stuffed friends came down from the shelf to snuggle on my bed.

Bill found Elly and me in the middle of them. I was hugging the biggest—a huge fluffy polar bear—and I must not have looked very happy for the first time in months.

"What's with you, Birthday Girl? You don't look very cheerful," he observed.

"She was just talking about Carl and Francine," Elly murmured, giving me a chin-up kind of look.

"Don't worry. They can't make any more trouble for you," Bill said, sitting down on the bed beside me.

"It's not that. I just sort of miss them sometimes."

"Huh?"

"They were good to me. They loved me, even if they didn't have the right to keep me." When I'd insisted on staying at the hospital, Carl had even sneaked back into my room, trashed it, and left a scary note, hoping I'd come away with them.

"I guess you're right," he sighed and put an arm around me. "But it's all so weird. Do you think you'll ever see them again?"

I nodded. "That's what I was just thinking. Francine's birthday is in two weeks. I haven't seen them since that last day at the hospital, but I think I'm beginning to forgive her for what she did. She only wanted a baby of her own. She picked me. It was wrong, but she did it for love, not to hurt anyone."

"Do you think Geringer . . . I mean, your dad, will let you go?"

"I hope so. He said they'd suffered enough, although they'll have to go to trial on federal charges of kidnapping and transporting a minor across state lines."

Elly sighed. "Can you imagine being on the run for that long? Because they had you, they never could stay in one place, keep a job for more than a year or so, or feel safe."

"No wonder they went bonkers whenever I asked to go on a field trip to Chicago or they had to take me to a doctor. They knew they were putting themselves in danger."

Bill gave me a warm squeeze. Leaning against his chest, I gazed up into his gentle eyes.

"I'm glad you came home, Stephanie," he whispered.

"Me, too," I murmured, smiling and breathing in the great guy scent of him. "Me, too . . ."

NICOLE DAVIDSON was born in Massachusetts and spent most of her childhood in Groton, Connecticut. She now lives in Maryland with her writing companion Katie, a Chesapeake Bay retriever who has a mind of her own. Ms. Davidson (who also writes as Kathryn Jensen) has authored twenty books for young people and adults since 1985. When she isn't working on a new book, she teaches writing juvenile fiction at Johns Hopkins University and for the Institute of Children's Literature. She is a member of the Author's Guild, the Society of Children's Book Writers and Illustrators, the Mystery Writers of America, and Sisters in Crime.

NIGHTMARES

HALL PASS
by Robert Hawks

Stumbling, Melissa cried out. The earth opened up and she fell in. Clumps of earth followed her, landing on her. She hit the bottom suddenly, striking something sharp which hurt.

At first she lay motionless, stunned. Then, with creeping nausea she realized... She was in a grave. Screaming, she scrambled for escape, clawing at the earth. She tore at clothing – not her clothing. Rotted fabric caught in her hands. Then hands reached down, and in her panic she grabbed them desperately, not even thinking who might be there.

"Easy," said the familiar voice. "Be quiet."

Don't be too sure *you* want to get out of class...

NIGHTMARES

DARK VISIONS
by L.J. Smith

"Read their minds. Steal their souls. Take your pick."

He was standing very still, every muscle rigid. His hands were shoved in his pockets, fingers clenched. And his grey eyes were so bleak and lonely that Kaitlyn was glad he wasn't looking at her.

She said evenly, "You're a telepath."

"They called it something different. They called me a psychic vampire."

And I felt sorry for myself, Kaitlyn thought. Just because I couldn't help people, because my drawings were useless. But his gift makes him kill.

DARK VISIONS
Book One: *The Secret Power*
Book Two: *The Passion*
Book Three: *The Possessed*

By the author of *The Vampire Diaries* and *The Forbidden Game* trilogy.

Order Form

To order direct from the publishers, just make a list of the titles you want and fill in the form below:

Name ....

Address ....

....

....

Send to: Dept 6, HarperCollins Publishers Ltd, Westerhill Road, Bishopbriggs, Glasgow G64 2QT.

Please enclose a cheque or postal order to the value of the cover price, plus:

UK & BFPO: Add £1.00 for the first book, and 25p per copy for each addition book ordered.

Overseas and Eire: Add £2.95 service charge. Books will be sent by surface mail but quotes for airmail despatch will be given on request.

A 24-hour telephone ordering service is available to Visa and Access card holders: 0141-772 2281